BLOODFLOWERS BLOOM

BLOODFLOWERS BLOOM

THE ASTRAL WANDERER™ BOOK TWO

D'ARTAGNAN REY

MICHAEL ANDERLE

DISRUPTIVE IMAGINATION

LMBPN Publishing
PMB 196, 2540 South Maryland Pkwy
Las Vegas, NV 89109

Version 1.00, May 2021
Version 1.01, September 2021
ebook ISBN: 978-1-64971-735-1
Print ISBN: 978-1-64971-736-8

THE BLOODFLOWERS BLOOM TEAM

Thanks to our Beta Team:
Rachel Beckford, John Ashmore, Larry Omans, Kelly
O'Donnell

Thanks to our JIT Team:
Peter Manis
Diane L. Smith
Paul Westman
Angel LaVey

If I've missed anyone, please let me know!

Editor
SkyHunter Editing Team

CHAPTER ONE

"Are we there yet?" Jazai asked as he, Devol, and Asla continued to walk down the winding road. The massive field of golden grass around them was the only thing they could see.

"Why are you the most childish one of the three of us?" the wildkin questioned in return as she pointed farther down the road. "There—in the distance. Do you see the forest?"

Jazai squinted, his expression somewhat offended. He formed a circle with one hand and peered through it as a soft glow of blue mana covered his hand. "Damn, how good are your eyes?"

"Are you using a cantrip?" Devol asked and looked over his shoulder at the diviner.

"Yeah." He nodded and moved his hand away from his face. "How is that surprising?"

"I didn't hear you use an incantation. I thought you had to say the cantrip's designation to get it to work."

"For the more powerful ones or those you aren't

familiar with," he explained and waggled his fingers in a parody of doing magic. "Anything you've done over and over, or simple things like using mana to light a wick, eventually simply become instinctive."

The swordsman nodded and considered his use of magic. "Hmm, I guess I have done that, but I thought of it as a trick, not a cantrip."

"I'm able to do a few without the incantations," Jazai stated and peered at the forest again. "Most are simple things like this spell—farsight. The one I use the most is blink, obviously."

"Both of those are transmutation spells, correct?" Devol asked and the scholar nodded in confirmation. He looked down the road at the forest far in the distance before he turned his head slowly to look at the other boy. "Have you had to look at things up close often?"

Jazai frowned and lowered his hand as he turned to address his teammate. "You've met Zier." He shrugged as if that fact alone provided sufficient explanation. "Well, let me tell you, that posh dryad often has me read passages repeatedly and he likes to talk for hours about something that can be summarized in two or three sentences." His teammates nodded in sympathy. "Is it a surprise that he would have me study things..." He jerked his head forward so he was only a couple inches away from Devol's, whose eyes widened instinctively. "Very, idiotically, close?"

The young swordsman moved back a little and nodded slowly. "Oh. Well, when you put it like that, I guess I understand."

"Your relationship with your mentor is rather concern-ing," Asla commented as she continued to walk ahead of them. "The fact that you seem to get so agitated over such trivial things is not healthy."

Jazai sighed, snapped his fingers, and blinked beside her. Devol had to lengthen his stride to catch up. "If it were only a few trivial things, I would let it slide. But it. Is. Every. Day. Asla!"

The wildkin frowned and she lowered her ear to shield against the irate magi's words. "I worry that you will lose patience and attack Zier one day."

The boy scoffed and folded his arms, his gaze fixed on where he'd seen the forest ahead. "No, I wouldn't do something like that." He grimaced and stared at the sky as if looking for answers. "I'm very sure that would mean he wins…something."

Devol jogged past them, turned to face them, and walked backward. "You know, I don't think we've come up with a plan for the mission. We should probably go over that before we get too close."

"We only have to deal with some flayers, right?" Asla asked. "It should not be an issue."

"I've seen a flayer in action," he told her. "About three months ago, when I was on my way to the order, I walked through a forest when I met Mr. Lebatt. He took care of it in a single strike."

"You can probably call him Vaust now," Jazai suggested. "We might be younger but even Zier and Wulfsun are younger than him by about a century, at least."

"We are supposed to be comrades in arms," Asla agreed as she held her gloves out and examined them.

"I guess so, but I think he likes it so it is not a big deal." Devol turned again to fall into step beside them.

Jazai shook his head and leaned closer to Asla. "Is he naïve or merely good-natured?"

"I think it is kindness," she answered with a slight smirk as she fixed him with a teasing look. "Is that a foreign concept to you?"

He rolled his eyes and leaned away as the swordsman stretched his arms.

"You know, it is rather unusual to find a group of flayers," Devol stated. He thought back to what he had read about them in the past and what Vaust had explained to him that day in the Wailing Woods. "They rarely travel in groups and are loners that prefer to keep to themselves."

"That is correct," Asla agreed with a nod. "In smaller areas, if there is more than one flayer and not enough territory to share, they will often battle one another for dominance."

"It must mean the alpha of this group is very strong," Jazai deduced. He opened his tome and flipped through the pages. "It is uncommon but not unheard of. There have been flayers so deadly that lesser flayers will go against their instincts and follow it when they have no chance to kill it or defend their turf."

"We should probably be more concerned, I suppose," Devol reasoned. "Even a young flayer can be vicious. How strong does one have to be to subjugate others?"

They continued to discuss what they knew of the creatures while they walked. When they were only a couple of hundred yards from the forest, a loud, frightful scream caught their attention. Asla bent forward and revealed her claws as her ears twitched. "Someone is coming."

"Someone?" Devol asked as he slid his hand to the grip of his sword.

A figure barreled out of the forest and ran toward them in a desperate, frightened dash to get out of the woods. The youngsters stepped aside but the young swordsman reached toward the man as he drew close.

"Excuse me, sir, but what happened in—" There wasn't a chance to finish his question as the stranger sprinted past them down the road. He uttered another fearful yelp before he raced out of sight. The three friends were baffled and they glanced at one another in confusion before they looked again to the place where the man had vanished around the bend in the path to the town.

The young swordsman had noticed cuts in his clothes and no weapon. There was not a chance anyone would go into these woods without one so he must have lost it.

"Did you...uh, get anything from him, Jazai?" he asked and gestured toward his friend's book.

The boy looked down and nodded quickly. "Yeah, he was easy. Either he didn't use his anima to protect himself or he was too frightened to care."

"He can run rather quickly without anima," Asla remarked as she frowned, her keen gaze fixed on the road where she could now see the stranger in the far distance where the road curved again.

"It looks like his name is Flynn and he is a member of a small hunter's guild in Malo," Jazai said, reading the information in his book.

"Malo—that's a couple of towns over from the village we got the request from," Devol remarked.

The scholar nodded again. "Yep. From what I can see,

they didn't send the mission to us immediately. The village put up a bounty first to try to deal with it. I guess his guild thought they could claim it if they hurried."

Asla shifted her gaze to the trees, "Are there others in the forest?"

"There were at the beginning," Jazai replied and closed his book. "The last passage says he is the only survivor—or as far as he knows, anyway."

The three teammates turned their attention to the forest again and studied it in silence for a moment. No animal calls or flayer screeches issued from the woods, only the gentle sighs of the wind that threaded through the darkness between the trees.

"So are we sure we don't want to have a plan before we head in there?" Devol asked.

"I assumed we would simply go in and kill them," Jazai responded with a nonchalant shrug and his anima flared. "But if you have something a little more detailed, I'm willing to hear you out."

The swordsman looked at Asla, who mirrored the scholar's shrug and activated her anima as she and Jazai began to enter the forest. The young swordsman sighed, drew his blade, and brought his anima out as he followed his two friends into the shadowy woods.

He had heard great tales of heroes going to vanquish foul monsters when he was a child. Now that he was a little older, however, it appeared that many of those stories were merely the grand retellings of a typical day in the life of an adventurer.

CHAPTER TWO

As the group pushed deeper into the bowels of the woods, Devol noticed something odd.

"I do not see any animals at all," he said and peered around him with a frown. "Even in the Wailing Woods, giant rats and things like that lived there."

"I assume these flayers either devoured or scared off anything else that lived here," Jazai reasoned. "It explains why livestock has been dragged away from the farms in the area."

"And people," Asla added as her ears pointed up. "We are close and I can smell a horrible stench."

The foul odor had caught the attention of Devol and Jazai as well. They pushed aside the brush ahead of them and entered a cleared area in front of a large den that had been cobbled together from wood, stones, bone, and various other miscellaneous objects. Everything had been combined effectively but somewhat untidily to create a huge cave-like structure.

"What in the world is going on here?" Jazai asked as he

opened his majestic. "Flayers don't make massive dens like this, do they?"

"Not normally," Asla agreed. She scowled as she looked at fresh blood that stained the grass. "They will either live in hovels or caves found in the areas they claim or make small dens suitable for only their use."

Devol studied the grotesque home of the flayers and took note of the bones that created the opening. Most seemed to be from animal carcasses, but he noticed several human bones twisted amongst those that formed the entrance. "This seems rather advanced for creatures like flayers."

"No kidding." Jazai sounded disgruntled as he examined the bestiary. "Flayers can make a glue-like substance with their saliva to help build their homes. But like Asla said, they are usually little hovels, not something like this. I would expect to see this being the home of blood mages or cannibals, not flayers."

"Cannibals eat their own, correct?" Asla questioned and gestured to a section on the left of the den. "It would appear you are not completely wrong, Jazai."

The boys shifted their gazes to where she had indicated. Two skulls were visible, and from their sharp features, they appeared to be skulls of slain flayers.

"Well, I guess they stepped out of line," Jazai murmured and closed his book.

Asla shut her eyes and sniffed the wind. She pulled a face of disgust before she opened her eyes again. "I smell death—both the scents of the long-dead and some that have only died recently."

Devol held his sword out. "Those must be the hunters.

Are any alive?"

Asla shook her head. "No, not from what I can tell."

"That's probably a good thing," Jazai remarked. "Can you tell how many flayers there are?"

"There are several scents, a few quite similar," she explained and attempted to cover her nose. "I assume those are the more lowly flayers and a much more noticeable stench almost masks them."

"Do you guys feel that?" Devol asked and lowered his blade slightly as he looked around. "I feel mana."

The other boy nodded. "I assumed it was the remnants of the hunters—their mana can linger for a little while, even after death."

"Maybe, but…" His thoughts were interrupted when a skittering noise issued from inside the den. The three young adventurers prepared themselves. It appeared their quarry was coming for them instead of the other way around. "So, will we still go with the simple plan?"

Jazai sighed and held his hands up. "If I knew a cantrip that would let me blow this horror to pieces, I'd go with that." He looked at the young swordsman. "Remember that fire of wrath you did against Koli during our first mission? Do you wanna give that another shot?"

"I've tried during training," Devol responded and shook his head. "I haven't been able to recreate it although I have been able to do other things."

"Yeah, I've seen the party tricks." The scholar chuckled. "They must have some value, I suppose, but I'm not sure what you'll be able to do with those."

"Quiet!" Asla ordered and crouched in readiness. "They are here."

They focused intently on the mouth of the constructed cave and a few moments later, four scrawny flayers stalked out. They were smaller than the one Devol remembered from the Wailing Woods—around six feet tall—and seemed to be underfed, which made the ravenous noises they emitted more understandable. The one in front of the swordsman hissed as it ran one of its boney blades over another to sharpen them.

"Four?" Jazai sighed, "If it was three, we could each take care of one."

Devol drew a deep breath as he lifted his blade and the light flared. The beasts screeched in surprise and he swung it in a deadly arc. The blade extended immensely before it struck the flayer in front of him. When the light dimmed, the creature twitched and jerked, then split vertically in two. Its companions shrieked with unbridled rage.

"That's much better than merely a party trick, eh, Jazai?" he boasted with a smirk.

The other boy chuckled and nodded to concede the point. "Fair enough. You got me there." He pointed to the remaining flayers. "But if you had slashed horizontally, you could have killed them all in a single strike."

He turned away sheepishly. "Well...sure, but you two would have been bored."

Jazai laughed but Asla frowned. "I think we would have been content," she muttered.

The creatures shrieked their individual challenges and surged into the attack. Devol turned into a head-on clash with one of the flayers and its bone-scythe arms struggled against his majestic.

The scholar blinked around the initial attack from the

creature that had focused on him and launched a missile of mana that hurled it back. Despite the force of the blow, it merely landed lightly and sprang toward him again. Rather than engage directly, he blinked into the branches of a tree and began to fire cantrips at the beast.

Asla caught the blade of the third creature with her gloves, turned, and flung it at a tree as her anima flared and the silhouette of a large, feral cat that glowed orange formed around her. She pounced closer to the beast and sliced at it with her claws. The flayer simply moved under her and the mana-enchanted strike felled the tree instead. With a groan and a flurry of splintered wood, it toppled into the forest.

This seemed to give Jazai's adversary the same idea. When two mana arrows pierced its shoulders, it extended its arms and cut the tree he perched in down with a wide, cross-cutting swipe. He jumped clear and yelled, "Shield!" as he fell toward the beast. A blue mana shield formed in front of him.

The flayer raised its blades but his shield blocked them as his feet connected with the creature and pushed off. He landed several yards away, turned, and pointed at the arrows. "Chains!" The mana arrows on its shoulders began to unravel, encircled its arms, and attached to trunks behind it. They held it in place and it shrieked and snapped its jaws as he approached it.

He held a hand up and whispered, "Blade." His hand was engulfed by the blue light of his mana and took the form of a short blade. The flayer continued to hiss and shriek at him as it struggled to free itself from the chains. The apprentice moved closer, swung his hand, and the mana-blade sank into its neck and beheaded it in one strike.

Asla dodged the third flayer with ease. While the beasts were known for their agile movements and quick kills with their natural blades, her seemingly malnourished opponent had almost no hope against the anima-enhanced wildkin. When it tried to slice her in two, she attacked first and severed its arms with her claws.

It cried out in pain as yellow blood spewed from the stumps. She took a moment to glance at Devol, who seemed to be using his target for training more than any real attempt to kill it.

She shook her head and returned her attention to her adversary. With a swift kick, she catapulted it toward the young swordsman. The creature collided with the flayer he was battling and surprised him as both careened past Jazai.

"What was that for?" he grumbled. "I wasn't in danger."

"I could see that, but this is not the time to play," Asla pointed out before she nodded at the scholar. "Can you finish them?"

The boy shrugged and held his palm toward them. "Fireball." An orb of flame formed in his hand and he launched it at the two collapsed flayers to ignite them both. They shook themselves briefly in an effort to extinguish the flames but the fire consumed them before they could escape the blaze.

"Won't that set the forest on fire?" Asla asked as the three friends watched them burn.

Jazai shook his head. "Not that it would be a bad thing, but cantrip flames don't spread like normal fire. Besides..." He lifted a hand and snapped his fingers and the fire immediately vanished. "I'm not such a novice, even if that were the case."

"I guess I can see why they were following an alpha," Devol said as he rested his sword against his shoulder. "They weren't as intimidating as I expected given what I remember reading about them."

"You have to keep in mind that they were terrorizing villagers," Asla stated. "To most people, even these smaller flayers are a deadly menace."

"It puts it all in perspective, huh?" Jazai said thoughtfully, his hands clasped behind his head. "We've become strong enough that things like this are simply a nuisance."

"We are gifted," Asla agreed with a nod, "but we should not get too comfortable. We must still deal with the alpha."

The three looked at the mouth of the den, knowing what awaited them inside. "I'm sure it is a big beastie and all that," the diviner said to end the slightly uncomfortable silence. "But it is still a flayer. Between the three of us, it shouldn't be a probl—"

A deep, massively loud cry issued from the den, one that each of the young magi could feel in their whole body. Asla raised her hands quickly to block her ears as the two boys simply stared, wide-eyed. When the scream died down, the silence in the forest became more palpable and the group realized what lay in store for them.

"That...didn't sound like it came from a normal flayer," Devol said and grasped his sword tightly. "That cry had something...terrifying to it."

"That certainly did sound like a big beastie, all right," Jazai muttered and lowered his hands to his waist. "So...uh, do we have a plan for this?"

CHAPTER THREE

"I do not believe the alpha flayer will come out on its own," Asla stated as she took one step closer to the cave. She hesitated for a moment and looked over her shoulder. "Should we proceed?"

Devol drew a deep breath. "We have to. It's our job." He flexed his fingers around the grip of his majestic. "But...uh, I have to say I would not guess that the noise we heard came from a flayer. Are we sure that's what is waiting for us in there?"

Jazai nodded, opened his tome, and studied the bestiary section. "It has to be, although I'm not a hunter or tracker by any means. Still, I've studied the more dangerous creatures for other magi many times and I've never heard of flayers submitting to other beasts. It has to be an alpha in there."

"Could it be a different species?" Asla inquired thoughtfully. "We are close to the border of the Zhangra empire. Perhaps they have a—"

"Flayers aren't in their lands," the scholar interjected

and flipped through the pages. "Or none have ever been seen there, at least. Even if they did have flayers, I doubt they would travel all that distance to here. We might be close, but we're still a couple of days away from the border and even longer for them."

Devol hefted his sword purposefully and walked forward. "Well, I guess the only way to find out is to take a peek," he reasoned and moved closer to the den. "You guys have my back, right?"

Asla nodded and straightened as she hurried to join him. Jazai followed and had begun to shut his book when the pages moved on their own.

"Hey, guys, hold on a moment!" he called as he opened the book again and his eyes widened.

"What's wrong, Jazai?" Devol asked as the two of them paused and looked at the apprentice. His gaze seemed transfixed on whatever lines he was reading on the page.

"I'm getting...something's thoughts," he stated with a glance at them.

"Some...thing?" Asla muttered in bewilderment. She and Devol returned to their friend's side and they huddled close to stare at the book. Inside was a half-sketched picture that consisted of the typical flayer scythe arms, a large body, and very little else. It didn't have the normal details Jazai's majestic typically showed when reading another person. Instead, a few words repeated to fill the entire page.

Hunt. Kill. Devour.

"This is coming..." Devol began and looked at the other boy in confusion. "Is it from the alpha?"

Jazai nodded slowly. "I mentioned before that my

majestic doesn't work on beasts, right?" he asked and both his teammates responded with nods. "Right. Well, I should probably change that to it normally doesn't happen. This is the exception."

"What could that mean?" Asla wondered. She turned to stare at the den and her ears twitched.

The apprentice shut the book and replaced it carefully on the side of his waist where it was secured with a leather strap. "Well, the reason it normally doesn't work on beasts is that my majestic reads the mana of my target," he stated. "Your mana is basically an imprint of your soul, so my majestic is able to sort through that and find memories. Animals typically don't have much mana. Some have more than others but usually not enough for my majestic to pick up on." He looked at the den, his concern evident on his face. "It would appear that it is different for the alpha."

"So for some reason, this flayer has much more mana than usual?" Devol asked. "How is that possible?"

"Well, the only way I can think of is rather...gross." The diviner scrunched his face at the thought. "But there have been times when certain beasts were able to increase their mana, sometimes by eating large quantities of mana-rich substances. Occasionally, they would feast on special fruits or even pieces of cobalt. But the most common way would be to...well, eat someone like us."

This gave pause to both his friends and they looked nervously at one another. "So if they eat a magi, they can also consume their mana?" the swordsman asked.

"Not merely any magi," Jazai corrected. "All humans, wildkin, fleuri, and realmers have mana, but you would not consider all of them magi and these mana-enchanted beasts don't roam the lands in droves. I don't think even eating an actual magi would be enough in most cases. My best guess would be that it ate someone with an anima."

"Ah," Asla whispered and flattened her ears. "I suppose that makes sense."

Devol looked at the bodies of the slain flayers. "I did not see any blood around their mouths when we fought them," he recalled. "I assume the hunters who were here before we came in were all given to the alpha."

"Most likely," Jazai concurred. "It probably needs more than only flesh to sustain itself now."

Devol turned resolutely toward the entrance and his anima surged. "Well, that means we have to eliminate it," he told them and held his blade up. "After all, if this creature is able to kill a magi with an anima, where does that leave the townsfolk or farmers in the countryside if we abandon them?"

Asla took a breath to calm herself and nodded agreement, but Jazai shrugged. "You make a fair point, but I am starting to realize that 'being strong' is honestly a pain in the ass."

"You could be helping Zier dust or something right now, you know," the wildkin pointed out.

He rolled his eyes and took a few steps closer to the den. "I guess I'd rather die valiantly than out of boredom. Let's get on with it."

Devol nodded as he and Asla followed. The wildkin took point quickly when they reached the mouth of the unnatural cave as her vision was best in the dark. "I'll be on the lookout," she stated. "Devol, if you can, keep the light of your majestic dim. It may give our position away otherwise."

"Or it could help to blind the creature," Jazai countered in a whisper. "If it is used to living in the dark like this, of course. I'm only saying keep our options open. This is new territory for all of us."

Devol nodded as the trio entered, all prepared to discover what this new creature was capable of and slay it as quickly as they could.

The den proved to be much deeper than they had originally thought when they saw it from the outside. It appeared more along the lines of a burrow and the ground sloped down as they walked. Devol looked at the ceiling of the cavern, where sticky gobs of flayer saliva were used to hold the ceiling in place. Not surprisingly, the remains of the inhabitant's meals were littered along what seemed to be the main path.

"Homey," Jazai muttered sarcastically and his eyes, which were usually soft and almost disinterested at times, were alert and scanned the area continually in search of signs of the alpha.

Devol moved to the front, the flat side of his sword against his chest to keep the light to a minimum. "Asla, do you have anything?"

"I can smell it," she stated, her voice low. "But amongst the rot of everything else here, I cannot pinpoint it. I can also hear…sickening sounds. It must be feasting."

"Perhaps it will be too full to offer much of a fight,"

Jazai commented and earned irritated looks from his teammates. "Fair enough. That might be a little dark given what it is probably feasting on," he admitted.

They reached a fork in the path. One led to a larger chamber and one to a small hovel. "I believe these are their living quarters," Asla stated. "The larger is for the alpha, of course." She sniffed the air and blocked her nose hastily. "Yes, it's down this path. I'm sure of it."

As Devol stared into the dark chamber, an idea occurred to him and he turned to Jazai, "Hey, if this creature is full of mana, we should be able to see that using vis, right?"

The diviner considered this in silence, but his eyes began to glow with his dark-blue mana. "I would say that is likely but I don't know for sure. This is my first time dealing with something like this."

The swordsman nodded and used vis on his sight. "I should have brought torches."

"Once we engage the beast," Asla said quietly and tapped his sword, "you will be able to use the light of your majestic more freely."

"I had hoped we could kill it in a sneak attack," he admitted as he looked at his blade. "Fighting in these relatively cramped conditions won't be easy for any of us."

The trio shared a silent look of agreement. "That would be preferable," she acknowledged.

"Who will attempt the killing strike?" Jazai asked.

"I will," the wildkin offered before Devol could say anything. "I am the fastest among the three of us and will have the best chance to get close before it can react."

The swordsman had intended to offer to do it himself

but she had a point. He nodded and turned to Jazai. "Then you and I will hobble it," he stated. "I'll blind it with the light from my majestic and you can tie it down with your chains."

"Got it," the boy said with a decisive nod. "Flayers are fast but not typically that strong. It would have a considerable struggle to break the chains, even with the enhancements it gets with mana."

Devol nodded as Asla extended her claws. With their plan in place, they entered the larger cavern and walked slowly and cautiously for about a hundred yards before Asla held a hand out and motioned for them to press against the wall. Devol crouched, narrowed his eyes, and peered deeper into the shadowy space. The alpha was about a hundred feet away and it was much larger than he had anticipated.

The creature did not have the scrawny frame of the flayers they had fought or even the alpha he had seen in the Wailing Woods. This one was tall—possibly eight or nine feet—but also broad with a massive carapace on its back that was wider than his entire arm span. It crouched in place and its only motion was when the head lowered and jerked up repeatedly. In the silence, the crunching sounds it made as it devoured its prey were unmistakable.

Devol turned away briefly and tried to not focus on the sounds. Asla tapped his arm and nodded to him. He looked at Jazai, who also nodded. They were ready and the beast was eating, which made this a perfect time to strike. He held three fingers up and counted down. As the last finger lowered, they all summoned their animas and raced toward the beast. The diviner blinked in front of them and thrust his arm out. "Chains!"

The alpha spun as a set of ethereal chains wound around its massive arms and head and pulled it back to expose its neck. The swordsman let his mana flow into his blade to illuminate the room and the flayer uttered an angry scream when the light burned its eyes.

Asla vaulted upward onto the flayer and drew her arms back. They glowed orange with her mana and she landed on its chest and sank her claws into the alpha's throat to slice through it. She jumped off as the chains released and the beast gurgled as it slumped heavily. The wildkin landed and the three adventures watched it twitch, the same question in each of their minds. Had they done it?

"What in the hells?" Jazai demanded as the alpha's head raised slowly. He pointed to the neck, where the deep wound had begun to close rapidly. "It's healing itself."

"That was a clean strike." Asla gasped and thumped a balled fist into her leg. "I should have tried to decapitate it."

"Worry about that later," Devol ordered as he held his sword up. "Be on your guard. It looks like its—"

The beast surged forward and despite its size, it could move as fast as any flayer. It drew its arms back and slashed them forward, but not at them. They stared as the creature targeted the ceiling. A little confused, it took a moment before they realized that the attack had begun to break the gooey substance and rock apart. As the ceiling crumbled, the chamber began to shake and the entire structure collapsed on top of them.

CHAPTER FOUR

Thinking quickly, Jazai grasped his teammates and blinked them into the divided chamber. They drew ragged breaths and stared at the path leading into the alpha's den, which disintegrated rapidly in the wake of the collapse. Fortunately, their area still seemed stable.

"It tried to crush us," Asla muttered. "That would make us almost inedible, I think, unless it planned to pick our remains out from the rubble."

"Well, it's not like it needed another meal soon," Jazai pointed out. "We have an additional problem, I think. The mana it has not only increased its physical stature but probably also its intellect. It recognizes us as a threat, or at least more important to kill outright than keep for dinner."

"Did it trap itself in there?" Devol asked and held his sword defensively as he stared toward the collapsed chamber. "Maybe it was too desperate to understand what it was doing."

The ground beneath them began to shake and they exchanged wide-eyed glances.

"Scatter!" Jazai shouted and they all leapt closer to the entrance. The alpha burst out of the ground, landed heavily, and focused immediately on the three young magi. "I guess we know what built the den now," the scholar quipped and pointed at the massive beast. Its dark, blank gaze settled on him. "Frost!" A blast of frigid air and ice left his palm, struck the beast in the shoulder and arm, and rapidly created paths of ice down the limb. He moved his arm to the side and used the frost to freeze the wall and connect the flayer's frozen arm to it to hold it in place.

Asla and Devol took the opportunity to attack as the beast began to carve the ice with its free arm. The wildkin targeted the throat once again to correct her mistake but was greeted by the razor-sharp fangs as the alpha turned its head to snap at her. She was forced to use a feint to move out of the way and the fangs only dug deep enough to inflict a light cut.

The swordsman had a little more luck and was able to slice a clean wound into its chest. Before he could drive his blade in, however, the alpha swatted him away with the back of its arm. The blow thankfully didn't cut into him, but the strength of the beast was enough to hurl him into the ceiling. He plummeted when gravity kicked in and it looked like he would fall into a sinkhole the creature had created, but Asla had recovered enough to quickly bound across and push him out of the way. They tumbled together and rolled out of range.

The beast finally freed itself from the ice. Jazai tried to counter with another cantrip but the flayer looked at him and uttered a high-pitched screech that forced him to cover his ears lest his eardrums burst. It swung both cutters down onto the magi, who extended his arms and called his shield. A large barrier appeared a second later and the alpha's arms struck it forcibly. The boy watched in shock as the shield only slowed the limbs and didn't stop them. He gaped as the boney blades of the flayer slid into and down the barrier. In a moment, though, he regained his senses and blinked to where Devol stood as the shield was destroyed.

He helped the swordsman up. "We're gonna need to try something different," he said bluntly as the flayer sharpened its blades with a determination that was somewhat disconcerting. "Or find a way to inflict real injury. Flayers are known for their ambush and speedy tactics, but this one fights like a likan."

"Both Asla and I were able to inflict some injury," Devol muttered and shouldered his sword while he observed the wound in its chest beginning to heal. "But it regenerates so fast. How is it able to shrug blows from majestics off?"

"Like I said, I assume it consumed a magi with an anima," Jazai reminded him. "From what I can see, it doesn't have an anima like we do, though. It's more like a magical coat around its carapace so it can take far more abuse and deliver it in equal measure, even against cantrips and majestics."

"It looks like Asla might have the right idea." The swordsman gestured to where the wildkin was able to dart between the legs of the creature and slash at its ankles. "It looks like she's trying to topple it."

"That will at least give us an edge," the other boy agreed and held a hand out as his mana flared. "You guys will have to force it down. I'll distract it."

Devol nodded and tightened his grasp on his sword in readiness. "Got it." He raced forward to join Asla while Jazai fired several missiles at the flayer, all focused on the arms and eyes. The creature began to thrash wildly. Asla rolled under the blows and Devol either leapt away or countered them. Although they were able to inflict numerous wounds on its feet and legs, they began to heal almost immediately. Both fighters eventually gave in to their frustration and used more mana than they normally would to each slice into the ankle of a leg and sever the feet.

The flayer fell and a burst of yellow blood spewed from the stumps. It thrust its blades down to steady itself as it peered at them and uttered another deafening cry.

"Would you shut up?" Jazai growled and waved a hand. "Pulse!" He blasted a wave of magical force that hurtled into the flayer's head and shut its jaw. His companions both lunged at its head to finish it, but the alpha spun with surprising deftness, swung its bleeding legs into them, and flung them away before it began to burrow into the ground.

"Dammit!" Devol cursed as he forced himself to stand as their quarry disappeared rapidly. He sighed. "We need to get out of the den before it comes back for us."

"Agreed," Asla said as she rubbed the bump on her head. "We'll have more space outside."

"To the hells with it," Jazai said in disgust as he marched past them. "I'll burn this den to ashes."

The young swordsman raised an eyebrow as the diviner blinked away. "It's honestly not a bad idea," he admitted to Asla as they raced forward. He took the rear and kept a watchful eye on the area behind them. They soon approached the entrance, where Jazai waited to set it alight, but the well-packed surface rumbled ominously beneath them.

"The flayer!" the girl shouted. Devol turned as something protruded from the soil and extended to reveal one of the alpha's blades. The beast seemed to slice through the earth toward them and the ground became unstable.

He managed to stop himself from sliding and held his sword out to prevent the creature's advance, but the blade simply sank into the soil without achieving anything. The flayer made no effort to engage him and the wild contortions of the dirt as it powered toward the entrance passed him without allowing him the opportunity to try to stop it.

"Jazai! It's coming for you!"

The diviner grimaced and jumped away a second before the flayer broke through the surface and the long limb carved at the air. The immolation cantrip he had prepared to burn the den was redirected toward the alpha instead. It defended itself with a deft spin on the now healed stumps and the fire struck the shell on its back. The creature made an odd keening sound and swung at Jazai, who leaned back as he blinked away, but the blade sliced into his chest before he disappeared. He appeared next to a tree, holding his bleeding wound.

"Damn it!" He grimaced in pain and leaned against the trunk as his mana snaked around him and began to close the wound.

Asla darted out of the mouth of the cave as Devol caught up. The tiger-like shadow of mana formed around her as she attempted a killing strike. Rather than move to dodge or block it as she'd expected, it spat at her and covered her in some of the sticky liquid that dotted the cavern. The glob struck with sufficient force to hurl her into a tree. In seconds, it had attached her to the trunk. She immediately began to fight to cut herself free, but that left only the swordsman to distract their adversary.

Even without its feet, the flayer had adapted quickly. It used its arms to fling itself at him as he sprinted out of the den and barreled its entire weight toward him. He held his weapon up and was able to deflect a blow from the alpha, but the impact dislodged the blade from his hand. With a desperate twist, he ducked under the beast and out of the den, but the creature plunged one of its blades into the ground and spun it to launch itself toward him and drive him off his feet.

"Devol!" both Jazai and Asla cried as the creature reared to kill the young swordsman. Even with death so close, however, Devol saw an opportunity. He held one of his arms up, seemingly to stop or slow the blow that arced toward him but instead, a flash of light emitted from his hand and the flayer's attack was stopped.

His teammates gaped at his blade that now protruded from the neck of the monster, having teleported back into his hand in time to deliver the blow. He tightened his hold on his sword grip and used vis to sear into the neck of the beast. It uttered one last, muffled shriek as he sliced through its neck and released a spray of blood from the staggering creature before it had a chance to behead him.

The flayer gurgled and its eyes narrowed as it began to twitch from the strike. Even with its enhanced regeneration ability, the wound was too deep to recover quickly. Jazai hurried forward and used a pulse to push it off Devol.

Asla managed to cut herself out of the goop the flayer had surrounded her with a second later. She vaulted onto the back of the beast, her claws raised. They shone with orange light and she swung them decisively to finish what Devol had started and sever the alpha's head in one swift motion. The creature's body immediately collapsed and she bounded off it as Jazai pulled Devol away before it could fall on top of them.

The three friends, ragged and with various wounds, looked at the corpse with disdain before the realization of their accomplishment dawned on them.

They had finally felled the alpha despite its enhanced capabilities.

CHAPTER FIVE

As reality began to sink in and the adrenaline started to wind down, Devol collapsed onto his back with a contented sigh. "Man. It's a good thing I knew about the weak point around the throat, huh?"

Jazai moved to examine a piece of the flayer that had been cut off during the attack. "I think you'll find that the throat is a weak point for most living things." He picked up a shell-like piece and studied it closely. "And it is more likely that you were able to fell the alpha thanks to your sword itself rather than swordsmanship."

He rolled his head to look at his friend. "What do you mean? The teleporting trick I did?"

The diviner shook his head and tossed him the piece he had been focused on. "That was neat but think about who you are talking to."

Devol caught it, removed his glove, ran his hand over the shell, and realized that it was a hardened piece of the carapace. "Is this from its back?"

"Nope. I saw it come loose when you cut into its throat.

This was protecting the trachea," the scholar stated and knelt beside him. "Your majestic is a powerful sword, far beyond an ordinary magic sword. Do you think you would have had the power to cut through that on your own from your prone position?"

Asla knelt on the other side and poked the shell. "The skin on the back of its neck was tougher but it did not have this shielding," she told them and tapped it thoughtfully. "I would think you would have to break it open with a blunt weapon first. Blades would only scratch it."

Devol looked from the shell to his majestic. "So you think this was due to the power of my majestic?"

The other boy nodded. "If it helps your ego, I'm sure it helped that you had the strength and intelligence to swing the blade in the right direction."

He frowned at his friend's sarcastic comment before he scrambled to his feet and threw the shell to one side. "Okay, I can't be too mad. It was certainly helpful to learn something new about the sword." He held the blade up for a moment and focused on the dancing light within it. "I guess it didn't register since it didn't brighten all that much."

"Well, you were preoccupied at the time," Jazai reminded him as he retrieved a small towel from his pouch and handed it to Asla. She accepted it gratefully when she realized she was still covered in some of the flayer's spit.

Devol nodded, sheathed his sword, and sighed as he ran a hand through his hair. "I suppose it is simply another thing to ask them about when I see them again."

"Who is them?" Asla asked curiously as she rubbed the towel along her arms.

"My parents," he told her as he walked away and pulled a brown sack from his pack. "But that is something for later. We should bag these heads quickly so we can start heading back."

Jazai nodded in agreement and fumbled in his coat for a bag before he glowered at the alpha's head. "I don't think any of us has a bag to fit that. Does anyone want to shove it into their backpack?"

Asla unclasped her cloak, shook it out, and handed it to him. "I believe we can bundle it in this."

"Are you sure, Asla?" the diviner asked as he took it tentatively. "I doubt that what will be left on it will wash out."

"I don't think any of this will," she remarked and gestured at her clothes and the grime and spittle still covering it. "I am likely to simply burn it all."

Jazai looked at the sticky yellowish liquid and made a slightly disgusted face. "That's probably the right choice," he conceded as he spread the cloak gingerly on the ground.

"I'm not sure if the two we burnt will count," Devol called as he used a large knife to sever their heads. "I suppose they are in one piece, though, albeit charred and crumbling a little."

"It's fine. We only need proof," Jazai responded as he and Asla lifted the alpha's head and placed it on the cloak. "Do you need another bag?"

"Yeah, throw it to me," the swordsman instructed. "Showoff," he muttered when his friend took one out and blinked it to him. He chuckled as he snatched it out of the air and placed the final burnt head inside it. As he checked to make sure the four bags were secured, he paused and frowned when a rustling from above caught his attention. He looked up quickly and moved one hand to his sword while the other held his dagger. It was unlikely that the noise had been an animal as they hadn't seen a single one other than the flayers since they entered the forest.

A moment later, a thought occurred to him and his caution turned to annoyance as he sheathed the dagger and shook his head, "Mr. Lebatt!" he shouted into the trees.

"Vaust?" Asla questioned as she tied the cloak over the alpha's head. "Is he here?" She stepped beside Devol as Jazai opened his tome.

"I heard something," the swordsman stated gruffly and his gaze scanned the trees. "I thought it was too good to be true that they would leave us to deal with this alone."

Asla sniffed the air. "That flayer's miserable stench is still obscuring my sense of smell, but I have not detected any familiar scents since we began our journey."

"It isn't surprising," the diviner said as he strolled up behind the two, his gaze focused on his tome. "It stands to reason that anyone who has been training with you has a very good idea how to get around your senses. But this one, in particular, would be an expert at it."

"So someone is here?" Devol grumbled and earned a nod from the scholar.

"Yep, and he is super proud that his pup is becoming such a fine warrior," Jazai said teasingly and looked at Asla.

"Pup?" she demanded before her eyes narrowed and her hair stood on end. "Freki! Get out here!" she yelled.

Another rustle issued from behind a tree across from them. The three looked in that direction as the wolf wildkin strolled casually from behind it. He smiled and waved sheepishly. Devol and Asla snorted annoyance and Jazai merely chuckled and shut his tome.

"Haven't I apologized enough, Asla?" Freki asked with a whine as his apprentice continued to give him the silent treatment. The group now walked along the path toward the anchor point that would return them to the Templar hall.

"Yeah, keep crying Freki," Jazai muttered and adjusted the large bundle on his back that wrapped the alpha's head. "I'm sure that will make her come around."

"It wasn't my decision. I trusted you and your partners completely," the wildkin Templar explained with a touch of desperation. "I was told by the grand mistress to accompany you."

"And as no one thinks to gainsay her, the excuse works well," Jazai remarked with a snicker.

"Why do they keep sending you guys to shadow us?" Devol asked with a glance at Freki, "I suppose I can understand the first mission as it was our first time together and we did not know what could happen. But we've trained and have run smaller quests on our lonesome. There should be some trust now shouldn't there?"

Freki sighed and when Asla continued to ignore him, he turned his attention to the young swordmaster. "There is. That's why I did not intervene, although I was about to when that monster had you pinned."

"I...appreciate the thought," he responded dubiously. "So you were merely on standby?"

"I was to be an observer," the wildkin said and folded his arms.

"Observer? What were you watching us for?" Jazai questioned with a baleful glance at the hunter.

"I cannot say," he stated, which of course earned him another look of ire from his ward.

"You should answer. I am curious as well," she said, albeit quietly and in a monotone that suggested she wasn't as curious as she was annoyed.

"Asla!" Freki exclaimed, thrilled that she'd broken her frosty silence, but she turned away and resumed her sulk. "I truly can't. The grand mistress asked me not to. I have probably already said too much but I'm sure she plans to tell you once we return."

"I'm beginning to sense that Miss Nauru is more mysterious than she lets on," Devol commented as they walked up a hill to a large tree stump.

"It comes with the title, I guess," Jazai said as he shrugged his bundle off and walked to the stump. He began to extend his hand but paused and looked at Devol. "Hey, do you wanna give it a try?"

The swordsman nodded, "Sure. I have it down now, I think." He placed the four bags on the grass and approached the stump, rested his hand on the top, and released a thread of mana. Several runes appeared on the wood and he immediately pointed to the one that would provide access to the Templar Order hall. He connected his mana to the rune and let it coat the symbol. As soon as he filled it, a small portal appeared and he continued to let his mana seep into the rune so the portal grew wider. He began to raise his hand slowly but maintained the connection so the portal would remain.

"Not bad," Jazai conceded with a pat on his shoulder. "At least you don't have to use your sword anymore."

"It was awkward using it as a giant key," he admitted as he picked the four bags up—a little tricky given that he still had to control the gateway, and the group hurried through. It shut as soon as he walked through and left no traces of the magi as the fields fell silent once again.

CHAPTER SIX

"Hey, guys, welcome back!" a joyful voice called as Devol exited the portal. He looked up and waved at Acha, a reptilian squama Templar he had gotten to know in his few months at the order. Alongside him was a human woman known as Reina—not all that talkative but a skilled swordswoman—and a dwarf by the name of Pete. The three stopped in front of the group and they all exchanged greetings.

"Hey, Acha. Are you guys heading out?" Devol asked.

The squama nodded and patted the daggers on his waist. "Yeah. We accepted a retrieval mission in the Osira kingdom."

Asla looked at him with concern. "Will you be all right in such a dry place?"

"He'll be fine," Pete said with a smirk and thumped a hand into the small of his teammate's back. "We made sure to pack extra water for that scaley skin of his."

Acha rubbed his back and nodded. "I'm not a red- or black-scale." He chuckled and tapped his cheek to highlight his dark-green scales. "So dry environments aren't my specialty. But Iguiza has dry climates as well. I simply need to stay hydrated."

"I have never been to your realm, but does Iguiza have anything like our deserts?" Reina asked.

He looked at her with a sharp-toothed smile. "We call the area that the black- and red-scales call home Ember Rock Plains. The heat there can reach almost boiling levels."

"And you can survive that?" she asked with a hint of shock in her features.

The squama's toothy grin slimmed to a more jovial look. "Well, not without the proper precautions—like my tunic." He stretched the blue fabric. "It's light and breezy but it has a special coating that keeps me cool. It's one of the few things I brought with me when I joined the order."

Reina shook her head as Pete chuckled. "Well, you could have explained that."

"It's a pity about Kanami, though," Pete remarked. Devol thought about the Tsuna scholar he had occasionally seen working with Jazai and Zier. "She badly wanted to come but the location is too much for her, at least for an extended stay."

"So you will be gone for a while?" Jazai asked.

Acha nodded. "Possibly. What we're looking for...well, we don't know much yet."

"What? Then how can you find it?" Devol inquired.

"We can certainly look for the signs." Pete laughed wryly. "The thing is, it seems it could be rather nasty. It is something magical, to be sure, and was found by an archeology team that came through one of their many ancient sites. The team disappeared, as has anyone who attempted to search for them."

"And you are not concerned that you are also now a team looking for them?" Asla asked bluntly.

"We will be fine," Reina assured them and placed a hand on the ornate necklace she wore. "My majestic will keep us safe."

"And mine will take care of anything in our way," Pete boasted and brandished the mace he had rested on his shoulder. It was almost as long as his arm and a round white orb on the end featured cracked markings that glowed orange. "We'll be fine and wouldn't have been requested if we couldn't handle it."

"Or at least have a good chance to deal with it," Acha added and tapped his daggers. "If it turns out to be a majestic, maybe I can claim it for myself."

"Potentially, but given the circumstances, you know what it is more likely to be," Reina replied.

He sighed and nodded. "Yeah, it's probably a malefic. Oh, well. Macha mentioned that there are a couple of majestics they are ready to test so I might have to check with her once we return." He looked at the Freki. "Speaking of which, you might want to check in with mistress Nauru."

The wolf wildkin nodded in agreement. "We were on our way to her. We've just returned from a mission."

"And this isn't getting any lighter," Jazai grumbled as he adjusted the sack on his shoulder.

"But why do you say that, Acha?" the hunter questioned.

"From what we were told, this isn't the only incident like this at the moment," the squama revealed.

"Aye, It seems a few of these odd anomalies have appeared," Pete continued. "And all at the same time. They started to come in before you left but in the couple of days since you've been gone, we've had almost double the number of requests for aid throughout the kingdoms."

"All of the kingdoms have similar occurrences?" Freki asked. His voice lowered as his eyes narrowed to show a more serious face that Devol only saw him wear once in a while. "And we have no clues about any of them?"

"We have many theories, all supplied by the clients," Reina replied with a shrug. "I'm not sure how much good they are. They all seem a little different."

"I see." Freki nodded and motioned for the younger Templars to follow him. "Best of luck to you three. We'll go and report to the grand mistress."

"Aye, good fortune to ya!" Pete called as Acha waved cheerfully and Reina opened the anchor point. The portal revealed a desert of golden sand and amber skies that the trio walked into before it shut. Devol turned his attention to the castle's main gate.

A mysterious force spreading around the kingdoms? Potentially dark magic of some kind involved? It sounded exciting!

"Hey, Heni, Coko! Are you here?" Freki called as they entered the main lobby.

"Coming!" a sweet voice responded. Two of the stewards of the order walked into the lobby from an adjacent room. Coko was a verte wildkin with the appearance of a white-and-brown spotted rabbit and Heni was a large, crimson-skinned daemoni man with curved horns who wore a double-breasted black suit jacket and slacks. "Hey there, Freki and friends. How was the mission?" Coko asked.

Heni eyed the wolf wildkin with curiosity. "I thought you were supposed to hide from your charges." The daemoni's voice was deep and booming but he spoke in a calm and polite tone.

Freki chuckled half-heartedly and nodded. "Yeah. I'm afraid I was discovered. But they completed the mission before they saw me."

The daemoni nodded and adjusted the collar of his suit. "The young Templars must be impressive to have discovered you at any moment during the trial."

"It wasn't as difficult as you might think," Jazai told him and swung his bundle. "Do you mind taking this, Heni?"

"This is the flayer mission from Brestshire, correct?" Heni asked as he took the bundle from him and lifted it casually.

"Yes, sir." Devol nodded and handed the smaller bags to Coko. "It was an alpha leading a few smaller flayers. Are you okay with them, Coko?"

"Oh yeah, no worries!" she said although, with her tiny frame, the four bags filled her arms and stacked on top of each other to obscure her face.

"We will make sure to send these to the clients," Heni stated and held the bundle at arms' length so the fluids that darkened the cloth didn't stain his suit. "I recommend you inform the grand mistress that you have returned, Freki.

Both to tell her of the success of the mission and to attend to a new development."

The wildkin nodded "Yeah. We ran into Acha and his team on the way in. They said something about anomalies popping up in all the kingdoms?"

"That is correct," the daemoni acknowledged with a nod. "Fortunately, the issue seems to be only on this realm so far. We are not quite sure if they are related, but the grand mistress has asked me to send all higher-ranked Templar to her whenever they arrive."

"We're on it." Freki and Heni bowed slightly to one another as the tall steward and his assistant wandered to the mailroom to transport the proof of the flayers' demise to the client. The wolf wildkin led the group to the main stairs. "Let's check in with Mistress Nauru and see about these new problems that are springing up."

Asla followed her mentor with Devol and Jazai a few paces behind. "I wonder if we'll be sent to investigate," the young swordsman said quietly to his friend. "I guess even if we are, it's not like we'll get to go on our own."

"That might be a good thing in this case," the diviner replied and chuckled at the confused glance he received. "Don't get me wrong. I was annoyed like you and Asla that they sent a handler to keep track of us. I'm simply better at hiding it."

"But you'd be okay if they did it again?" Devol asked. "I thought we were hoping to get out on our own."

"There is a difference between having faith in us and throwing us to the wolves," Jazai warned as they began to ascend the stairs. "Having someone watch over us while we dealt with a few flayers is a little insulting. But if they sent us to look into something at our skill level when they don't even know what it is? Hells, I think we would be better off in a thieves guild."

"Do you honestly think it could be something that bad?"

They reached the top of the steps and continued along the main hall to the grand mistress' chamber behind Freki and Asla. "You heard what Acha and the others said, right? Those archeologists disappeared and anyone sent to look for them."

"Yeah? I thought the Templars were who you called to brave the unknown," Devol retorted.

Jazai smirked and nodded. "You still have that spirit. I would have lost a bet by now," he said but mostly to himself. "You are right in a way but remember how most people see the Templars. Maybe a few centuries ago, we would have been called in as soon as something like this happened, but now?" He drew a deep breath and looked him in his eyes. "Now, it means they have run out of options."

CHAPTER SEVEN

When Freki pushed the doors to the grand mistress' room open, Devol felt like he had walked into the middle of a council meeting. Zier and Wulfsun were present, along with Vaust, surprisingly. The boy had seen him come and go since his arrival and unlike the other elder Templars present, he was not one of the mentors, which meant he had either invited himself or they had indeed interrupted a rather dire meeting.

"A timely return, Freki." The grand mistress' voice seemed to drift through the room. The swordsman finally located her where she was almost hidden behind Wulfsun's massive frame. She wore dark-blue robes. "Ah, and the young magi are with you."

"Of course, mistress," the wolf wildkin said with a small bow. "They performed admirably during their mission."

"I would expect so," Vaust commented from where he sat on a large chair with his feet kicked onto a pink ottoman. "They were able to detect you as well."

Freki frowned slightly. "Perhaps I merely decided to

accompany them on their return after the mission."

"Nah. He slipped up after we killed the flayer alpha," Jazai interjected and held his book up. "It turns out he's a sucker for a happy ending, especially when it comes to his ward."

This earned him a tired and somewhat exasperated look from the wolf wildkin and an irate one from Asla, who pushed Freki forward.

"We completed the mission, Madame Nauru," she explained without preamble. "We were told that there have been some interesting developments since we departed?"

"Interestin', sure." Wulfsun snickered. "I prefer my interestin' things to be more jovial and less evil-soundin'."

Nauru closed her eyes and nodded slowly, "Yes, some rather unfortunate events are taking place around the kingdoms, but we will return to that in a moment." She glanced at the wildkin mentor, whose blue eyes glimmered under the shade of her hanging garden. "Tell me, Freki— how did they fare on their own?"

He glanced at Jazai, who gave him a mischievous grin before he shook his book again in response. The hunter waved him off as he approached the head of the Templar Order. "They took care of it, madame, and as you can see, gained a few small wounds to boot."

"Although with a flayer alpha, one good strike is all it takes," Zier interjected and his apprentice scowled.

"It was a mana-infused flayer too," Devol added and drew the attention of all present, "Jazai said it might have eaten a powerful magi or something. Honestly, it took a fair amount of work to kill it."

"Is this true?" the dryad asked and looked at Freki, who

nodded. The old scholar tapped his chin in amusement. "So not only an alpha flayer but an awoken one as well?"

"Awoken?" Devol asked and glanced at the apprentice. "Do you care to translate?"

"It's merely the designation they give to beasts and critters that can access mana," Jazai replied. "Like I said, every living thing has mana but it doesn't mean it can use it well or even use it at all. Animals, in particular, aren't exactly known for it outside a handful of creatures in the Osiris and Soel kingdoms. The idea is if they do find a way to access mana, even in rather unfortunate ways, they've 'awakened' to it."

"It's typically not a wonderful thing, given that the most well-known method to achieve this is by devouring a mana-user as your flayer friend did," Vaust added and seemed thoughtful as if he sifted through his memories. "Although I do recall coming across an awoken stag once in my travels in Britana. I don't know how that happened, but it could bloom flowers in its wake."

"It sounds enchantin'," Wulfsun commented and stroked his beard. "I didn't think that would make an impression on ya. Doesn't Avadon have loads of awoken beasties?"

"Oh, certainly," Vaust replied with a smirk. "They are nasty little creatures, especially those that eat the purps and flowers we use to make our enchanted wine." He held his gourd up with a smile as he popped the top. "It leaves less for me and it's also why we keep our forests to a minimum outside the Scarred Valley."

"Moving on," Zier interrupted grumpily and turned to the grand mistress. "I suppose we should show a little more faith in our protégés—as you have, Madame Nauru. If we had made a bet, we would all have to pay."

Wulfsun coughed as he slid his hand into his satchel and handed two cobalt shards to the mistress. "Speaking of…"

The dryad's eyes narrowed. "How do you keep any cobalt for yourself?"

"I win some bets. I'm not a complete idiot." The man snorted as he folded his large arms.

Before the scholar could retort, his gaze returned to Nauru. "Wait—you bet with him?"

"I don't recall," she replied and frowned at the shards. "I think it might be the fact that I simply didn't say no."

Wulfsun shrugged and held a hand out. "I'd be happy to take those back, madame, so you don't need to fret about taking part in such a nasty habit as gamblin'."

Nauru looked at the shards for a moment before she tucked them slowly into her sleeves. "No, it is quite all right, Captain. I'll simply consider this your tithe."

The Templar's brow furrowed in confusion. "Tithe? Are we a parish now?"

"You've lived here your entire life, Wulfsun. You should know she's playing you," Vaust chided teasingly and took a sip from his gourd. "Although I suppose I could also be wrong. If that is the case, I should be more concerned. I take pride in my ability to speak blasphemy quite fluently."

Devol approached his friends as the others continued to make jokes and snide remarks at each other's expense, with the exception of Nauru. The swordsman folded his arms as he watched the display. "So I assume this means it isn't that much of an emergency?"

"Huh? No, this is fairly common." Jazai flipped through his tome before he sighed and shut it. "Their animas are up. Anyway, even in dire situations, they are likely to joke and such. You have to be comfortable with a little gallows humor around here."

"I think the only situation that would truly get them riled up would be if someone knocked our gates down," Asla added and pursed her lips in thought. "Although maybe that is not a guarantee either. They might find it amusing."

Nauru looked at the young magi and nodded to them in sympathy before she held a hand up to silence the others in the room. "You can continue your little squabbles another time, gentlemen," she stated and folded her hands into her sleeves. "We should return to the matter at hand but first, with the completion of their mission, the young ones should now know what could potentially lie in store for them."

Freki and Wulfsun shifted uncomfortably, Zier locked eyes with Jazai, and Vaust merely glanced at them as he took another sip. All three youngsters felt an odd chill at the sudden shift in the mood in the room

"Is something fatal involved?" Devol asked when no one seemed inclined to speak.

"Potentially," Zier responded and drew an angry stare from Wulfsun and growl from Freki before Nauru held her hand out to stop them.

"This seems rather a jump," Jazai stated and studied the faces of the elder Templars. "You don't trust us to do a mission alone but now you are putting us in a situation that could potentially end our lives?"

"Well, the mission you completed could have ended that way," Nauru pointed out and took several steps forward toward them. "And you need not worry about this now, young magi, but with your completion of this mission—one with a red mark—you have now completed two missions that can qualify you for a challenge that can potentially open not only this world to you, but almost all the realms."

While some of what she had said flew right over Devol's head, her last statement certainly caught his attention. "What do you mean, madame?"

She paused and looked up at her garden again. "You all have your reasons for being here in the order. Not all by choice, necessarily, and perhaps a couple of you are not completely sure where your road will lead. With that in mind, we have been testing your potential." She turned, moved toward her desk, and opened one of the drawers.

"We already knew you were all gifted in your individual ways," she continued. "But even the finest sword is no use if it simply rests on a mantle. The missions and quests we have had you do over these last three months since the day we brought you together for that first retrieval mission were not without a particular purpose. It was to see if you could qualify for a challenge that makes even great warriors and skilled magi shudder to participate."

She turned toward them again and held some type of badge or signet up. It was a jet-black spiral shape with the only exception being a shining silver diamond in the center that stood out even more against the deep black of the object. "Tell me, have any of you heard about the Oblivion Trials?"

CHAPTER EIGHT

Each of the three young magi had different reactions to Nauru's query.

Jazai stared at her in surprise bordering on shock, as he had indeed heard of the Oblivion Trials and very little of it was good.

Asla was frozen by trepidation. The trials sounded familiar to her but she couldn't place from where. However, when she saw the reaction from her mentor as his apprehensive gaze drifted from her to the grand mistress, she realized that whatever it might be, it was nothing to be taken lightly.

Devol's response was almost nonexistent. He had no idea what this trial was, only that it seemed to rattle almost everyone in the room. Vaust seemed fine, although not either of his usual reticent or snarky selves. The boy raised his hand and stepped forward.

"Um…I don't know what those are, madame," he admitted. "But if it's another mission or something, can I request that we go alone this time?"

Jazai caught him by the shoulder and pulled him back a couple of steps. "You might want to hold off on that for a minute, Dev," the apprentice warned in a hushed tone. Devol noted this was the second time the diviner seemed hesitant to take on a challenge. He was no coward and was usually as interested in having more freedom as he and Asla were, but he also seemed more aware of the lines they shouldn't cross quite yet. Things had certainly become far grimmer since they returned to the order, he thought and focused on the grand mistress.

Nauru seemed to understand the confusion and placed the sigil on her desk. "I suppose it was a silly question to begin with," she reasoned and walked closer to the three friends. "Even if you did know of the trials, it would probably be through rumors and such, which can provide quite a skewed perception of the event."

Jazai relaxed slightly, folded his arms, and nodded. "Ah, okay. I was worried these were the same trials that I heard ended fairly gruesomely."

She nodded at him. "Indeed, that would be downplaying it."

Jazai's face fell and he stared at her in stupefaction. "Pardon?"

"The Oblivion Trials are rather gruesome throughout," she explained with an unnatural calm given the topic. "Not only in the finale. But that is part of the reason why I wished to discuss it with you." She wandered to the foot of her bed, sat, and beckoned them closer. "You are all still young and your path in life can still take many directions. With that in mind, I decided that while you are here, you should have an opportunity for an option that would let you expand outside the order if you wished to do so."

"By participating in an event that you acknowledge is typically a bloodbath?" the apprentice questioned. He looked at Devol, who remained silent and merely listened to the conversation to see where it went. His gaze drifted to Asla, who was looking away, lost in her thoughts. "I guess I can appreciate the idea behind the thought, but I'm beginning to think this was dreamed up by Zier trying to get rid of me."

"Nonsense, Jazaiah," the dryad claimed, his head held high. "How would that benefit me in the long run?" The boy frowned at his mentor, not quite sure what to make of his reaction.

"Yes, the Oblivion Trials can be rather harrowing," Nauru acknowledged. "However, do you know the reason why people seek out the trials?"

This time, it was Devol who answered. "I assume there is some great reward to be won?" He pointed to the badge on the desk. "That object looks valuable."

"It is indeed," she confirmed. "That is known as the oblivion marker. It is given to those who pass the trials. Typically, only a small number are given out each year—ten at most—and they are prized among adventurers for what they can do for them."

"Are they some kind of rune or trinket?" Asla asked, now focused on the conversation again.

"It is a badge, one that grants access to many things for the owner," Nauru explained. "You see, the trials were established an exceptionally long time ago. They were devised by three royals from the kingdoms of Renaissance,

Britana, and Osira when the other realms were first discovered. The purpose of the trials was to find adventurers, soldiers, and magi who were willing to brave the realms to discover what lay inside."

"Oh, I know about that!" Devol exclaimed when he recalled a little history his mother had taught him. "The Grand Arkadia Tournament was named after the world as a whole to signify unity. They still hold that to this day with all other kingdoms as well."

"Correct," the grand mistress said with a nod and a bemused smile. "Although these days, it is a tournament to strengthen bonds between the kingdoms as well as build personal kingdom pride. The first was established as a secret test for the three great kingdoms to find those strong and brave enough to venture into the unknown. It became a separate event afterward."

"So these Oblivion Trials are run by the kingdoms?" Asla asked and scratched her neck, her face scrunched in thought.

"Not quite," Wulfsun interjected. "They are run by a separate council now, which is made up of members from all kingdoms and even several realms."

"Have you ever made the attempt, Wulfsun?" Devol asked.

The Templar captain nodded, slid his hand into his jacket, and produced a badge that he held out for the trio to see. "A handful of us here in the order have. In fact, a few of that number are in this room."

Freki retrieved his marker from the front pocket of his jacket. Vaust whipped his cloak over his shoulder and pointed to his marker that was attached to his tunic and almost blended into the dark fabric. The three young magi looked at Zier, who simply shrugged. "I had no use for one."

Jazai rolled his eyes. "Well, it makes you stand out at this moment."

The dryad nodded. "Perhaps, but it is something to consider as Madame Nauru continues her explanation. You may know the trials by reputation—one that is rather grim. Do consider the possibilities she is about to tell you about but also consider if they are worth it to you."

Devol looked at the grand mistress. "What does one of these markers do?"

"They allow a freedom most cannot find in not only the kingdoms but several of the realms," she stated. "The reputation from the trials is well earned and as such, great weight is carried by those markers. If you have one, I am sure any guild in the kingdom would be willing for you to join them at your request. They act as passports for travel to any kingdom and several of the realms. You will be given access to numerous special storehouses and inns for supplies and shelter and have the opportunity to take on secret missions—ones that bring rewards of great riches that can only be taken by those with oblivion markers."

"You could also simply sell them," Wulfsun admitted, flipped his in the air, and caught it. "Many collectors would pay more than their weight in cobalt to have one of these. I'm not sure why but the jewel in the middle of the marker is diament. It is another one of the few materials that can harness mana." He held the badge again out and let a trickle of his mana flow into it. The jewel created silver lines around the darkness of the black material and formed into a rose-shaped pattern. "It only reacts to the owner's mana, even if it is stolen or traded, so it's not like they can get any use out of them. But some people simply like having rare things, I suppose."

"And on top of that, they give you a fair amount of leeway with the law," Vaust continued as he tucked his cloak into its usual folds. "Those secret missions can also include political ones or even sanctioned killing. As such, there are certain things those who have a marker can get away with without recourse, thanks to special sanctions given to those who succeed in the trials."

"Which is part of the danger," Nauru admitted. "The trials today include more than only adventurers and soldiers. Thieves, assassins, dark magi, and many more often enter, looking to gain a badge for sinister reasons. You will compete against them for one of the markers should you choose to pursue this course."

Devol nodded and considered everything he'd heard before he asked, "What would we have to do? You said we were only nearly there, right?" Asla and Jazai seemed similarly interested if more uneasy about the prospect.

Nauru looked at Wulfsun, who nodded as he put his marker away. "That is correct. Although it was not intended, your first mission together became what is known as a red-marked mission due to the circumstances. This was also true for the one you completed now."

"I see," Asla said. She glanced at Freki, then Vaust. "Is that why you sent observers?"

"Indeed, although in the case of the mission in Roux-woods, that was simply because of the contents of the package. We did not know about the thieves who wanted to acquire it." The grand mistress spoke with a hint of sorrow in her tone. "But we want one more test to confirm your preparation and…well, for assistance." She turned to them and rested a hand on Wulfsun's shoulder. "And this time, you will not be shadowed. Instead, you will be under the command of the good captain."

Wulfsun looked at the three friends with a massive grin.

Jazai ran a hand through his hair and sighed in frustration. "Well, I suppose that is one way to make me prefer being watched. Being babysat."

CHAPTER NINE

"So Wulfsun will be leading us?" Asla asked and looked at her mentor, whose eyes narrowed at the Templar captain. "Are we his soldiers then?"

"You are my comrades, as always!" Wulfsun declared. When they regarded him dubiously, he shrugged and opened his hands expansively and somewhat apologetically. "It is only that...well, the current circumstances are peculiar and I have the most experience in our little troop."

Devol folded his arms and fixed the man with a look that bordered on contempt. "When I asked to be your apprentice, you gave me the run around when I thought you would be on board. What changed now?"

The older Templar grumbled and shook his head. "This isn't about that, lad! This is about the mission and assessing your skills in the field." He smiled encouragingly and nudged Nauru. "And remember what one of my conditions was?"

"You gave me several," Devol recalled.

Wulfsun rolled an eye, "The big one, lad. The one I said I couldn't overlook."

"Oh, right. Permission from my parents." The boy sighed and recalled the rather in-depth conversation the two had on the topic when he brought it up. He thought that since they had sent him to the Templars in the first place and he was only a year away from being able to enlist in the guard without permission, he should have the authority to make large decisions like joining the Templar Order on his own. Wulfsun, however, was adamant about that particular point and it was one he had yet to take care of between the training, quests, and missions.

"Right you are!" the large man declared. "But should you join me on this mission, you may have a chance to zap two critters with one spell, as it happens."

"What do you mean?" Devol asked and glanced at Nauru for an explanation.

She beckoned to Zier, who retrieved a small box. He opened it and a large map appeared in mid-air to display the land of Renaissance. It shifted to focus on the city of Levirei. "This is where we got the mission request from," she explained as the map changed to a massive ethereal depiction of the city. The large, spiraling tower in the center known as the Star Seeker Tower stood prominently in the image. "A lord from the town requested our aid in a matter that would be most shocking under normal circumstances, although we have become quite used to it over the last few days."

"Which might be an issue in and of itself," Zier noted.

"There has been some mystical disturbance in a valley

not far from the city's borders. They have not been able to discover what caused it or even what it is."

"Is it the same thing Acha and the others are investigating?" Freki asked.

"I cannot say for sure but similar descriptions were given by completely different sources." She extended a hand and moved the map to a large black patch. "It is some kind of dark magic and has either killed or incapacitated any who have attempted to dispel it or enter. In all areas, the best they have been able to do is contain it in a variety of ways but no one has managed to snuff it out."

"So...do you think it is malefic-related?" Jazai asked and when a few gazes settled on him, he raised his hands cautiously. "I'm not trying to spook anyone. All I'm saying is that seems to be one of the more logical theories. If this was simply basic dark magic or ritual gone wrong, there are many specialists who could take care of it. Outside of perhaps a few cities that like us, there would be no reason for anyone to call on us for this."

Zier, although possibly a little annoyed at his apprentice's frankness, could not exactly disagree. "Malefic, blood magic, or a wicked entity are the current guesses."

"Wicked?" Devol asked and drew a curious look from Asla as well.

"Basically a cursed person or creature," the young diviner explained. "Rather like the awoken but generally of an even worse disposition. Usually, blood, dark, or abyssal magic is involved."

"Abyssal magic?" Wulfsun murmured and stroked his beard. "I hadn't thought of that. It would make some sense.

Does anyone want to bet on it?" This was met by groans and chuckles throughout the room.

Devol raised a hand. "I think you might have a problem, Wulfsun."

The captain sighed and waved a hand to dismiss the suggestion. "In any case, it's all hands on deck right now. All experienced Templar are heading out to check on these things. We've had about nine different mission requests to look into 'dark happenings' of some kind over the last few days all across Arkana. And since they are 'undiscovered' missions, that means they are black-marked."

"Before you ask, Devol," Vaust interjected and drew the boy's attention, "I assume you have yet to have someone explain a mission's ranking system?"

"I have not been told anything but I can guess that it is similar to the missions my father would post for the other guardsman." The young swordsman counted off using his fingers. "Green, yellow, and orange. Green missions meant they were simple and quick and orange were difficult and dangerous. Guards could earn extra coin if they took those missions that were outside the city, generally joining military soldiers."

Vaust nodded, a satisfied smirk on his face. "Very similar, yes. But for guilds, it is a little more expansive." He held a hand up and spread his fingers. Five small dots appeared above them and all except the one over his pointer finger turned a different color. Devol guessed it was due to a transmutation cantrip. Starting from his pinky, it went green, yellow, orange, red, then black. "We have two extra colors as you can see—red and black. Red is the most difficult, typically, which is what the missions you have done so far have been classified as."

"Okay..." Devol said, a little surprised that they had been able to complete the most difficult missions themselves now that he thought about it. After a moment, however, he shook his head. "Wait—you helped with the first one."

"Correction, I saved you during the first one," Vaust responded and closed his hand. The mana spots disappeared. "But you all did well and I can't take that from you. And before you get too excited about your last mission"— he looked at the wolf wildkin—"Freki, even though it was a red-marked quest, how would you rate it?"

"Eh, orange at best, no stars," Freki replied casually before his gaze snapped to Asla and he assumed a fretful expression. "Erm...maybe one star?"

"Stars?" Devol interjected. "Is that another marker?"

"Indeed Like I said, our system is more nuanced." Vaust held three pale fingers up. "Missions have a color and either no star or up to three. This is to help with planning and building teams and all that. Also, it increases the price for the clients, so you want to make sure you know what you are asking." He leaned back in his chair and swished his gourd. "I asked Freki his opinion because as a hunter and someone who has been on numerous missions, he has a much better grasp of the difficulty of certain tasks. Sometimes, you get lucky and are given a higher marked mission that is easier than expected."

"It seems a little dishonest to take advantage of that," Devol remarked and Jazai slapped a hand to his forehead.

"I will never haggle with you around," he muttered.

"Same here." Vaust chuckled, "You are a noble one, aren't you, Devol?"

"I think it is an exemplary show of character," Nauru stated calmly in an attempt to bolster the boy.

"Of course you would. You are the grand mistress of the Templar Order," Vaust replied and took a sip. "It would be bad form for you to think otherwise."

"And it is not the same for my men and women?" she retorted and her eyes narrowed at the mori, their blue depths smoldering.

"Of course it is," he stated with an easy smile. "I'm merely the exception. My specialty is killing, after all, so what's a little scheming on top of that?"

She sighed and brushed him off. "Please remember we have young ones with us and set a positive example," she muttered and turned to address the three friends. "Black-marked quests can be the most difficult but if they have no stars, that typically means we have no confirmed details for them. In such cases, they are automatically marked black and are only able to be taken by the most experienced members of guilds and mercenaries. That is the reason why this will be an official mission for Wulfsun with you as his subordinates."

"Young comrades," he corrected, his gaze on Devol, "Although we may have to put that on paper for practical reasons."

"Okay, I understand all that," the swordsman acknowledged and held two fingers up. "I have two questions, though."

"Go ahead," Nauru told him.

He lowered one finger. "So if we complete this mission, we'll be sent to the trials?"

She shook her head. "This is a final observation to see if you would qualify for the trials in our eyes. Technically, you could take part in them if you happened to stumble upon them."

"Pardon?" Asla asked but the woman remained silent and merely gave her a small smile.

"Okay, then," Devol said, shrugged, and lowered his hand, "Then can we get back to what Wulfsun said before?"

"What about?" the captain asked and frowned as he tried to recall what this might be.

The boy pointed to the magical map. "You said this could 'zap two critters with one spell.' I assume one of the critters is getting this qualification from you, but what is the other?"

The man looked at the map and nodded. "Ah...right! I almost forgot to mention that." He looked at Nauru, who granted her permission with a nod for him to continue. "Well, boy, we have no anchors that take us directly to Levirei, so we'll have to take a train there."

"A train?" Devol inquired and understanding lit his eyes. "What—oh. A train would take us through—"

"Aye, lad." Wulfsun smiled broadly. "We'll take the train to Levirei from your home city, Monleans."

CHAPTER TEN

Far away from the order, in a darkened forest in the corner of the Britana Kingdom, was an old, neglected manor that had stood for more than three centuries. At one point, it was a prized abode, built by an earl who had made a fortune selling specific curios during a fad period all those years before. He had only lived in the house for a few years and was eventually driven away by his paranoia, or so the townsfolk from the nearby village said—or at least they did when they had lived there. The village had been abandoned a good many years earlier.

It was in this darkened mansion that Salvo stood, his jaw clenched as he shut the front doors behind him and walked into the main lobby. Dark wood, rickety floors, and a few vases and statues left behind when the earl had fled his home created a dismal scene, most of them in various states of disrepair. He walked past the curved stairs and into a long hallway, although he paid little attention to his route. Resentment seethed within him as he considered what he should do next. Ever since the failed mission, he had been given busy work—tasks meant for the under-lings, not him.

But it wasn't only pure frustration and feeling cheated that made him so bitter. If it were only that he would have simply burned the manor down and left his employer, although he had almost done exactly that on a few occasions. For once, his annoyance was eclipsed by something else—disappointment in himself. He felt he had let down one of the few people—perhaps the only person—he respected more than himself.

Footsteps ahead intruded and Salvo's instincts were still keen enough to snap him out of his brooding. He looked at a familiar face, although it seemed foolish to call it that given that the person it belonged to could change it on a whim. Koli strolled casually up the hall and smiled at his partner in amusement.

"Well, hello there, Salvo," he said cheerfully as thunder cracked outside. "You missed the rain. Good fortune seems to be following you."

"Like a geist, Koli." he retorted, his voice low and harsh. "Are those maniacs in?"

"Do they ever leave?" his partner responded and held his nose for a moment. "I'm beginning to wonder if hygiene is a foreign concept to them."

Salvo shrugged and prepared to move past. "It makes no difference to me. I'm only here to pick up spare bodies."

Koli raised an eyebrow. "Is that so? You have good timing. The next batch won't be here for a few weeks from what I understand. Are you going somewhere?"

He stopped and straightened as he fixed the trickster with a firm look. "I am done simply waiting for orders and being the others' errand boy. I'm going to go and find them, Koli."

"Oh. You're showing initiative. Who are you looking for?" As much as Salvo's current demeanor simply begged to be prodded, he was genuinely curious at what plan his former partner's mind had concocted over these last few boring months.

"The ones who took the box," Salvo stated and clenched his fists as he shoved his hands into his pocket. "Those damned Templars."

Koli nodded. He had assumed it would come to that eventually. "Is that an order from your glorious leader?" This was answered by something sharp and warm that poked at his cheek. His partner had produced his wand, Kapre, and pointed it at him with a shaking fist.

"Do not mock me or him, Koli!" he insisted and small sparks of flame flared from the red jewel at the top of the wand. "And don't be so arrogant. You had the box and lost it. You couldn't even handle a few brats so I will not listen to you prattle on about your—"

"If you recall," Koli interrupted as he slipped a hand under his eyepatch, "it was my partner who was the first to retreat." He raised the eyepatch to reveal his malefic. "And, as much fun as it would have been to have a chance at the mori, a rather interesting development occurred during my fight as well."

Salvo hesitated and the sparks faded from his wand as he growled and put it away. "Yeah, that majestic blade. You told us," he muttered. As much as his rage fueled him, his better judgment still won out. He couldn't fight Koli on his own and especially not in a place like this. "Whatever.

Leave it be. I'll have my chance to see what it does for myself." With that, he attempted to leave again but his companion reached back and caught his sleeve.

"Tell me, do you have a plan to find them?" he asked, "or will you simply spend a good while walking the lands in a big game of hide and seek?"

Salvo yanked his sleeve away. "I'll start burning things and get their attention. Maybe I'll start with Rouxwoods where we saw them last."

Koli chuckled. "I admire your tenacity, but that's more likely to draw in far more than only the Templars, if they show up at all."

"So be it," the other magi retorted. "I need to release some anger anyway, and if that doesn't work, I'll eventually think of something else once I've cooled down."

"Cooled down?" The trickster continued to snicker. "There's a better chance of the Astrals returning than that happening, Salvo. Even in your state, you must realize that."

"What's it to you?" Salvo snapped and spun to face him. "You've run odd jobs since the failure the same as I have. I haven't seen you doing anything to help look for them."

"I was not asked to," Koli stated, his tone matter of fact. "I'm on contract, unlike you. In fact, I made a delivery to our dear friends down below that will finish my term under your lord's employ. I had hoped to run into you at the estate, but it seems fortuitous that I run into you now."

"Is that so?" the fire magi muttered and shook his head. "I know you are playing coy, Koli. You have at least some idea of what he plans to do. Why bother leaving? You are paid well and once he changes the realms, what good will it be to not serve under him?"

Koli frowned and pulled his eyepatch down. "I still have my freedom of choice, Salvo. No one will strip that from me," he replied, his gaze calm and deliberate. "That was something we both held dear at one point."

Salvo's eyes narrowed behind their shades. "Who says I don't? But even I can see the inevitable. I guess I learned that no matter how far above fate you think you are, it finds a way to slap you back into reality."

The assassin studied the man he once believed he knew and felt somewhat disappointed. But in spite of that—or perhaps due to the time they had shared—he decided to offer him some aid. He reached into his tunic and retrieved a device. "Here, take this."

"An a-stone?" The fire magi took it and examined it curiously. "What? Is this for us to stay in touch?"

"You know I'm not that sentimental, Salvo," Koli teased and held a finger up. "During that little scuffle in Rouxwoods, I did one small thing to be safe. I planted a rune—a tiny one—that let me attach a trace amount of mana onto it to open a small line of communication, which would allow me to listen to anyone speaking within the vicinity of the box."

"What?" The other man gasped. "And you didn't tell anyone?"

"I told your boss," he said with a smirk. "I let him decide whether to tell others. I guess he chose to keep it to himself."

Salvo grimaced but looked at the a-stone. "How much longer will the rune last?"

"Oh, not long at all at this point," Koli admitted with a shrug. "A day, maybe a little more. As I said, it was rather small so it would not be discovered easily. Fortunately, the contents of the box seemed to obscure it for the most part. But that's not what you should be concerned about." He pointed at the a-stone and circled his finger. "I heard something quite interesting before I arrived. It appears your quarry is preparing to leave on another mission. They intend to go to Levirei to investigate some disturbance there."

"They are?" his partner asked, his eyes wide as the smallest grin began to form on his lips. "When?"

"In a day or so. You can listen to the conversation for yourself. The mori won't be with them, it seems. Another Templar named Wulfsun will lead them. And it appears they are investigating dark, ominous magic that has been springing up throughout all the kingdoms. It seems Alastair is getting things going now, huh?"

Salvo's eyes widened even more. "He's already beginning? No, this must be one of the tests he mentioned."

"I would think so. It's causing quite a fuss, whatever it is, but it's hardly something that will bring down kingdoms and empires." Koli smirked. "Do with the information what you will but hopefully, you won't be so sulky from now on."

Salvo certainly was not. He was now genuinely smiling as he rested a hand on the trickster's shoulder. "I knew there was a reason why I kept you around."

"How sweet." Koli chuckled and ran a hand through his violet locks. "Listen, Salvo, since I'm on my own again and have time to kill, I suppose I could accompany you one last time if you like."

The fire mage removed his hand from his shoulder, his smile still present, but he shook his head. "No, I gotta do this. I want to do this on my own. Unless you want a rematch yourself, I don't need you to intrude in my fun."

He shrugged good-naturedly. "Fair enough. Are you sure you can take on another Templar on your own? I'm sure this Wulfsun has a majestic as well."

Salvo moved his jacket aside and unclipped a box from his waist. "Despite what you may think, Alastair still trusts me." He produced the box and showed it to the assassin.

Koli's eyes narrowed before a bemused grin snaked onto his face. "I see. I guess he was saving that experiment for a different time?"

"Either that or he realized it could be more useful in my hands," the fire mage replied and put the box away. "I'll get a few more tools from the freaks. After that, I'll listen to what you gave me and be on my way."

"I see." He nodded, turned away, and headed out of the hall. "Then I wish you well in your hunt, Salvo."

"Where will you go now, Koli?" he asked. "Will you simply wander around causing a little slaughter on the way?"

"Not precisely," he admitted and slid his hands into his pants pockets. "I also heard something interesting for me in that conversation—something I had thought about doing for a while and well...I have the time now."

"Then I guess I wish you luck in whatever the hells that is," the fire mage told him, now so enthusiastic that he almost skipped down the hall that led to the basement stairs.

Koli reached the doors to the main entrance and opened them to glance at the rain that poured outside. "You should probably save that for yourself, Salvo," he whispered as he set off. Lightning flashed above but not a drop of rain fell on him. "Even if you are victorious against the Templars, I do not believe you have chosen wisely when it comes to a free future."

He stared at the sky. Another bolt of lightning streaked through the wide expanse and the white light reminded him of the light from Devol's majestic. He smiled when he thought of it. "And that may lead to me doing something rather naughty."

CHAPTER ELEVEN

Jazai opened the door to the roof of the center spire, his personal area where he would go to think when things became too heavy for him. He had forgotten that it was not exactly unknown and was also no longer only his.

"Evening, Jazai." Devol looked over his shoulder at the apprentice as he closed the door. "Have you come to think?"

"I guess I could talk instead," he responded as he walked to the swordsman's side and leaned against the railing. "Are you thinking about the Oblivion Trials?"

"Eh?" his friend muttered, his attention focused on the stars. "That seems a little far off to worry about now. I'm thinking about the mission."

He regarded his friend with a mixture of confusion and amusement before he turned and looked at the stars with him. "I'm curious about something, Dev."

"What's that?"

"Don't take this the wrong way although admittedly, I'm not sure how to phrase this so it doesn't sound mocking." He glanced at him and hesitated slightly before he continued. "How are you so naïve about the wider world? You grew up as the son of a guard captain in Monleans, the capital of Renaissance, and were taught by your mother who was schooled in one of the finest academies. You aren't exactly a farm boy from a tiny village."

Devol's response was simply a good-natured chuckle and a shrug. "I realized that myself on the Rouxwoods mission, if you recall." He looked a little sheepish. "I guess it was because I was so focused on being in the guards that all my training was put into that. You still have to go through a couple of years of physical and educational instruction in the guards, so learning more about things outside of kingdom history—math, and sciences, schools on bestiary and such—all that could wait until then. I'm not sure if my mother or father are aware of things like malefics and the Oblivion Trials. I assume they might be. Perhaps they hoped I would never have to worry about them."

Jazai laughed dryly, "Poor luck for you, it seems."

His friend responded with a slightly goofy smile, "Maybe, but in a way, I was still taught right." He tapped the hilt of his majestic on his back. "I may have not been in the know about these kinds of things, but I'm prepared for them nonetheless. It's something I should thank my parents for when I see them again."

The young diviner nodded and thought briefly of his father. "You haven't seen them since you arrived, have you?"

"No, but I've sent them letters." He shook his head with a self-deprecating smile. "I've left out some of the more intense things. My father might be amused by our missions but my mother may be a little more concerned."

"They sent you to train with the Templar so they have to know something like that would happen," the apprentice responded. "Although you were certainly sent downriver damn quickly."

"It's the best kind of training if you ask me," Devol retorted with a laugh. The door to the spire opened again and they turned as Asla stepped out. "Hey there, Asla."

"Good evening." She shut the door and joined them at the railing. "I like this perch, Jazai."

The magi nodded. "I liked the peace," he said with a sly grin. "But the company is appreciated too."

"We were talking about the upcoming mission," Devol told her and hopped up to sit on the rail. "And about the trials later down the line."

She nodded and tapped her claws on the metal. "Yes, I've thought about that too."

The young swordsman folded his arms and looked from one to the other. "Both of you seem worried about those."

"Well, yeah," Jazai stated flatly. "It's a nice gesture, I suppose, but I have to admit that taking part in the Oblivion Trials was not something I contemplated personally until today."

"It can't be that bad, can it?" Devol asked. "Almost all the mentors have completed it."

His companions both sighed. "True, but they also completed it when they were older. I believe Wulfsun and Freki were around twenty years of age when they attempted it. I am unsure how old Vaust or the grand mistress were, but potentially centuries," Asla explained.

The apprentice shook his head. "Honestly, even the experience that comes with age doesn't automatically guarantee victory. I've heard that many older magi—even those from other realms who vastly outlive humans—have fallen in the trials."

"Really?" The swordsman seemed unconcerned as he returned his focus to the stars. "I understand if neither of you wants to participate. It is a big risk. But I have to admit I'll be lonely without you."

Jazai stared at him, his expression one of confusion, and he moved closer to him and leaned against the railing. "Wait—what? You've already decided? I thought you said it was too far away to worry about right now."

Devol shook his head. "Oh no. I made my mind up before we were dismissed from the meeting. I merely think it's too far away to be troubled by it at the moment."

Asla hopped onto the railing and steadied herself on the balls of her feet. "Might I ask what makes you so confident, Devol? Do you truly not understand what awaits you in the trials?"

They waited in silence while he considered the question. "Well, I suppose I don't, not entirely, but isn't that the point? It's supposed to be mysterious, isn't it?"

Jazai looked like he thought he might be dreaming and should slap himself out of it. "Yes," he said finally, "but the one thing you do know is that there is a very high mortality rate."

"The same could be said about the mission we are about to do," Devol replied. "In this case, we know people have either died or simply disappeared and we aren't sure what is causing it other than some vague dark magic. That isn't stopping any of us from taking the mission, is it?"

His companions looked at one another and their surprised expressions acknowledged that he had made a good point. "Fair enough," Jazai began, his face pulled into a thoughtful frown, "but that's different. For one thing, Wulfsun will be with us and he—"

"We've hoped to not be followed by an elder Templar while on a mission," Devol countered before he could finish. He seemed a little bored as he began to do a handstand on the railing, "Unless you were more comfortable facing those flayers and that giant creature in Rouxwoods because you thought we had backup."

This also surprised the other two, who realized that perhaps they had suspected, albeit not consciously. If anything, Devol would probably have been the only one, at least on the first mission, who truly believed they were alone, even if Asla and Jazai only vaguely thought of it in the back of their minds.

"That's quite astute of you Devol," she responded.

"Thanks, but I'm not trying to discourage you at all." He raised one hand and balanced on the other. "I'm glad Wulfsun is coming with us, both because I want to see him in action and I take it as a sign that they are putting their trust in us. If I joined the guard, I would be under the supervision and the orders of others for years, even decades. We're undertaking a mission that requires a Templar of Wulfsun's ability to be at the head. That's exciting, right?"

"From your point of view, certainly," Jazai remarked

with a casual grin. "But I get you. It strokes the ego if you think of it like that."

"I'm curious, Devol." Asla went into a handstand to mimic him. "What do you hope to gain by competing in the trials? As mistress Nauru said, you can earn a place in the Templar in time. If it is your path—and similar to mine—to aid them, aren't the trials superfluous?"

"Not at all," he said confidently. "It allows me to do more so much faster. And there are those missions I can do with only one of those markers. I see it as a challenge." He placed both hands on the rail and flipped off to land on his feet. "People keep saying I'm gifted and all that but I've heard of gifted recruits in the guard and army. Some simply live a normal life and those who truly stand out show they are gifted by accomplishing things few others can. I suppose if I want to prove not only myself right but also everyone else who believes in me, I need to do something similar."

His words left his friends speechless. Asla climbed off the railing as he put his hand out in a similar gesture to the first time the three had stood on this balcony. He gave them a reassuring smile as they held their hands out and placed them on top of his and returned his smile. The moment lasted mere seconds before they departed and headed to bed. Jazai and Asla might still have doubts, but they now felt similar to Devol. They merely had something else to accomplish first.

CHAPTER TWELVE

"All right, lads and lassie! Rub that sleepy dust out of yer eyes. It's time to get this mission underway," Wulfsun shouted from across the bridge as Jazai, Devol, and Asla wandered out of the gate. Beside him stood Nauru, Vaust, Freki, and Rogo, surprisingly enough, who waved eagerly at them.

"Morning you three." He greeted them warmly and Devol noticed his second, lower pair of arms cradled a bundle of something wrapped in cloth. "I got word you guys were heading out on a big mission led by none other than the illustrious Captain Wulfsun."

Vaust shook his head as he tapped the large Templar's chest plate. "There are a number of things I would call Wulfsun but I'm certain illustrious is not one of them."

"Ah, come off it, Vaust. He's only telling it like his heart feels," Wulfsun boasted, clearly delighted by Rogo's proclamations. "But moving on from me for a moment. Rogo the smithy here has fashioned a few little trinkets for ya."

"Trinkets?" Asla asked and looked at the bundle with interest. "Something with runes?"

Rogo waved one of his larger hands. "Nah, that's not my expertise at the moment but I am rather good with majestics. I've been working on these since your first mission and thought it would be good to give you guys some options in the field just in case."

He unwrapped the bundle and approached the young wildkin. "First for you, dear Asla." He withdrew a miniature crossbow with strips on the bottom that he undid to bind them to her gauntlet. "This should give you ranged options. I know you are fast but sometimes, merely shooting things is smarter, you know?" He produced a pouch, handed it to her, and pointed at his waist. "There is about a dozen bolts in there and you can load up to three in the crossbow at once. The enchantment on the weapon lets you control the trajectory of any arrow you fire from it after its shot but only temporarily. The arrows have a little cobalt dust on them, which empowers them to punch through other missiles and even weaker spells."

Asla nodded as she examined the crossbow. "I like this," she told him with a soft smile. "Thank you, smithy. I will make sure to care for it."

"Not a problem." Rogo smiled, turned to Jazai, and retrieved a rather intricate piece of jewelry. Five silver rings were chained together by their sides to form a single item and he handed it to Jazai and motioned for him to put it on. "I had help from the dwarves with this one. They are better at handling magic in crafting," he explained and pointed at the ring on the boy's middle finger. "You can bind cantrips onto each of the rings. Then, you only have to point and send a trickle of mana into that ring and the stored spells will activate."

"Truly?" Jazai marveled at the trinket. "That's quite handy. I'm glad Zier isn't around. He would probably say that gets in the way of me learning to use the spells without incantations."

"Ah, you'll have time to train for that, but you're heading out into the field now," Rogo exclaimed and tapped the rings again. "The dwarves told me you need to form the spell around one of the rings but not cast it. This binds it to the ring for you with the power you grant it."

"I see." The diviner focused on his pointer finger and exhaled a slow breath as he mumbled something. The ring glowed momentarily with his blue mana before a rune in the shape of an explosion appeared. "It's a missile cantrip," he explained and pointed to a rock. The ring flashed and two fist-sized missiles launched, streaked into the rock, and destroyed it. Jazai nodded with a satisfied grin. "Much appreciated Rogo. I can certainly get some use out of this."

"My pleasure," the smithy said with a thumbs-up. "But remember that you have to reset the spell after each use." He pointed to the ring and the diviner noticed that the sigil had gone. "Think of it like bullets in a gun. You gotta reload." The boy nodded in understanding as Rogo walked closer to Devol and studied him for a moment. "You were an interesting one to craft for, I gotta say, buddy."

"I was?" Devol tried to peek inside the cloth. "What did you end up making?"

"Well, I first considered something long-range like Asla's crossbow, but that didn't seem practical given the size of your sword and all." Rogo slid his hand into the folds of the cloth. "I've been watching you train. You can do some spiffy things with that majestic but it doesn't look like you've mastered it quite yet."

The young swordsman sighed and nodded. "I can do a few things but that is about right."

Rogo patted him on the shoulder. "Buck up, buddy. I'm sure you're at the cusp. But it made me think. You should still have a trick or two up your sleeve you can rely on for now so..." He pulled his hand out of the cloth to reveal a dagger in a small sheath. The grip was black with a cobalt pommel and a few odd etchings in a ring around it. "I fashioned this little beauty."

He handed it to Devol, who unsheathed the dagger. The blade was made from truesilver, said to be one of the materials that could withstand magic and wound some rare beasts. It gleamed even in the dim light and displayed a clear reflection of his face. "It's beautiful, Rogo," he said, amazed. When he clenched his hand around the grip, some of his mana pooled into the cobalt. "What the—"

The smithy chuckled, took the blade in his fingers, and lifted it. He tossed it several meters away where it dug into a rock. The boy looked at him incredulously before he began to walk forward to retrieve it, but Rogo stopped him when he caught hold of his jacket.

"Ah, hold on a moment," he said and wagged his finger. "You didn't think I gave you a regular dagger, did you? This is a two-for-one. It'll help with close-quarters battles, but try to reach out for it and connect with the mana in the cobalt."

Devol extended his hand and used vello to snatch the handle of the blade before he was somehow dragged over to it. "Whoa!" he exclaimed from where he appeared next to the dagger and pulled it from the stone. "It lets me blink?"

"It's faster than blinking," Rogo proclaimed and smiled at Jazai. "At least for most people. That cobalt has your mana tucked into it, so you merely need to call to it and you'll appear next to the dagger. Nothing can stop ya." He tossed the empty cloth over his shoulder and clapped briskly "That was probably the trickiest to complete. Macha helped with it—oh, speaking of which, when you guys return, she wants to see you all and get you outfitted with proper armor."

The three young magi looked at their garb. Beyond some light chainmail Devol wore under his jacket, none of them exactly had armor to speak of.

"I am grateful but I am not sure if that would work for me," Asla responded cautiously and shifted her feet a little. "I prefer to be light so running isn't hindered."

"Yeah, me too. Being weighed down can lead to complications with some spells," Jazai agreed and looked at Rogo. "Like blinking."

"Not a problem," the smithy assured them with a smug grin. "Macha knows something as basic as that. You merely have to work with her and she'll fashion something that will keep you protected and that's to your personal tastes."

"That sounds great." Devol nodded enthusiastically, flipped the dagger, and tossed it at a point close to the smithy's feet before he warped to it and took one of his hands. "It's much appreciated, Rogo."

"Eh, don't mention it. This is what I do, after all," Rogo stated and shook his hand. Devol picked the dagger up and sheathed it before he attached it to his belt as he and the others joined Wulfsun.

"All right. Are we heading to Fairwind?" Devol asked.

"Fairwind?" Nauru asked. "Why would you start there?"

"Isn't that the closest anchor to Monleans?" he responded and recalled his adventures on his journey to the order. "That's where the map led me."

The grand mistress smiled gently, turned to the large rock filled with various portal runes, and pointed to one near the middle. "The map you used was a little old. It is true we unfortunately lost an anchor point near Monleans a few decades ago, but we wouldn't let it remain dormant forever." The rune activated and a portal opened to reveal lands very familiar to him beyond the gate.

For once, he felt peeved although still slightly elated at the familiar sight. "Honestly, I wish I had known about that before I came here."

"Think about the memories you made along the way, not the inconvenience." Nauru laughed, stepped to the side, and ushered them through. "Be safe, all of you. They are in your hands, Wulfsun."

"And they will be very safe with me," the captain declared, picked a large knapsack up, and stepped toward the portal. "All right, you three. The real adventure begins now."

CHAPTER THIRTEEN

Devol exited the gateway onto a field of wavy green grass and ran forward until he had to stop on the edge of a ridge. His home stretched before him, bounded by longstanding marble walls, spires, and towers that surrounded the central castle. The large structure gleamed as the sunlight caught the jewels and stained glass windows that displayed moments in the history of the kingdom of Renaissance. He was a little surprised that it was so visible even as far away as he was.

After being gone for so long, it was probably the first time he was ever truly amazed by Monleans, the capital of the kingdom.

A sharp whistle sounded behind him as Jazai approached and stared at the panorama with him. "Man, it's been a while since I was last here."

"So you've come through before?" the swordsman inquired and his teammate nodded.

"Yeah, a long time ago with my father." The diviner

smiled. "I could barely handle cantrips then. I was very young."

"It's breathtaking, isn't it?" he remarked and smiled again at the city in the distance. "You know, Jazai, I don't think you've talked much about your childhood and where you came from."

The boy shrugged. "Well, I moved around often so have many different stories. But I was raised in Quealva for the most part." He pointed behind them to Asla and Wulfsun. "But that's something for later, don't you think? You're the guide again this time since you know the area best."

"Not a problem." He turned and waved at the others. "Come on, guys. I know the fastest entrance into the city so it shouldn't take any time at all." He bounded off the hill and used a little vis to cushion his fall before he raced on across the plain.

"The lad is mighty excited." Wulfsun laughed and stroked his beard as he absorbed the sight of the city. "It's best to not lag too far behind. The process to enter the city can be time-consuming." With that, he leapt off the ridge and pursued the swordsman as he yelled at him to slow down.

"Process?" Jazai checked his robes before he took out a small blue book and opened it to reveal his identification papers. He sighed with relief. "So Zier did slip it to me. I would have forgotten, which is dumb of me given that I should be used to this." He looked at Asla's comically large travel bag and smiled. "I'm sure Freki put your papers in there somewhere?"

She sighed and nodded. "It's in the lower left pocket. He gave me a thorough explanation," she admitted and hoisted the backpack. "Well then, let us go." With a flare of mana, she bounded off the ridge and caught up to the other two quickly. The diviner put his book away and blinked after them.

Fortunately, Devol's knowledge and possibly his position as the son of a guard captain was indeed a big help as the small team was able to enter the capital with little effort. As they proceeded, the boy pointed out the sights, from a watch tower that was said to be the place where a great general directed the Monleans army from during an attempted invasion a couple of centuries before, to the garden district that was favored by many magi as a relaxing area to study their practices. He then took them through the Monleans' trade market, the biggest in all the kingdom. It was there, as he showed them some of the fashionable wear in the capital, that a familiar voice called to him.

"I know that tenor," Devol said with a smirk as he looked around and waved at an approaching figure in white-and-gold armor. "Captain Castiel!"

The others noticed a rather young man with long blond hair and fair skin and an inviting smile who waved in response. He approached them quickly and placed his hands on his waist as his smile widened. "I thought it was you, Devol. It's good to see you back," the guard captain said cheerfully. "Were you ever able to find the Templar Order you set off for?"

He gave him a playful frown. "Do you think I've been running in circles these last few months?"

"It's a possibility," Castiel retorted with a wry grin that took any possible sting out of the words. "You've always been more gung-ho than thoughtful in my experience."

"Well, you should have a little more faith, good sir!" he chided as he placed a hand on Jazai and Asla's shoulders. "These are my friends, Jazai and Asla. They are recruits in the Templar Order like me."

"A recruit?" Castiel asked, momentarily astonished. "And here I thought you were dead set on being a guardsman."

"I did too if I'm honest," Devol admitted and pointed at Wulfsun. "But I think I can do more as a Templar. This is Captain Wulfsun. He'll be my mentor."

"You might want to hold off on that declaration for a wee while longer, lad," the man chided but he chuckled as he extended a massive hand toward Castiel. "A pleasure. I'm Baioh Wulfsun of the Templar Order."

Castiel took his hand and studied him with a mixture of surprise and awe. "Baioh Wulfsun? I never thought I would ever meet you. My mother has told me stories of you."

"Your mother?" the large man questioned, his eyes wide with confusion and a trace of concern. "Who would that be, Captain?"

"Corrin Gale. She told me stories of her time in the Templar," the guard revealed.

"Corrin!" Wulfsun shouted and caught the attention of several people around them. "Then yer her son? My word. Has it been so long that you've grown up to be a guard captain, no less?"

The younger man grinned and nodded as he reached behind him. "Indeed. If you would like more proof…" He withdrew what appeared to be a lamp, a winding metal cage of gold where a glowing orb hovered in the middle. "She passed this down to me."

Wulfsun was taken aback when he saw the guard captain's majestic. "Fyrehart. Well, I'll be…" he said wistfully. "I never thought I would see it in action again. It's good to see it still fulfilling a duty."

"I always try to make her proud, sir, and her comrades as well," Castiel replied and put the lantern away. "She always speaks fondly of her time in the order."

"Aye, she was always warmer than any hearth for us, especially during the dangerous missions," Wulfsun said with a smile. "When she left to have you, we all missed her greatly. But given the kinds of things we have to deal with, it was better that she cut all ties and started anew. Although I suppose if she's passing stories along, we haven't completely faded from her heart."

The guard captain shook his head and his eyes seemed a little misty. "Not at all, sir. I wish I could take you to her but she moved to Britana a couple of years ago. She said she missed the air there."

The Templar nodded knowingly. "Aye, I was rather surprised to hear she'd decided to settle in Monleans, but I guess going to her homeland right away would have been something of a tip-off. Why didn't you go with her, lad?"

Castiel shrugged and looked at Devol. "Well, while Britana is her home, this is mine. Once she passed her majestic on to me…well, I was fast-tracked into the captain position. I couldn't leave my people."

"I'm glad you stayed, Castiel," the young swordsman interjected. "Things would be much less fun without you."

The captain chuckled and nodded. "I do have to admit, it's been somewhat dull without you to chase around. So are you coming to visit?"

"I'm on a mission," the boy revealed and glanced at his teammates who looked questioningly at him "Uh...we're on a mission. But I want to say hi to my parents while we are here. Is Father on duty today?"

Castiel shook his head. "It's a day off for him. Unless he had plans today, he should be home with your mother."

"Good, then let's go there now." Devol beckoned excitedly to the others. "It was good to see you, Castiel."

"Don't be a stranger if you come through again, Devol," the guard captain shouted and waved as the small group began to head to the Alouest abode. Castiel looked at Wulfsun. "It was an honor to meet you, sir."

"Likewise, young Gale," the Templar replied and nodded in the direction of the lantern. "She shines with you. Fyrehart can be picky and it's not only genetics that can let one wield a majestic."

"Thank you, sir." The younger man fidgeted slightly. "Although there is one thing, sir—two, in fact."

"Go ahead, lad."

"Do look after Devol. He can be rambunctious and perhaps a little childish, but he has a good heart and strong sword arm."

Wulfsun snickered. "Trust me, I've seen that."

"And the other..." He looked around warily. "I'm sorry to bring this up but do be careful about the Templar signifier. Monleans has a better history with the order than most, but there are still those around who are...spiteful." He looked a little worried and like he hoped he did not offend.

Wulfsun gave him an easy smile and a nod. "Don't worry, lad, I know the score. But I appreciate the concern."

"Come on, Wulfsun!" Devol shouted over the noise of the crowd.

"I'm coming!" he responded and nodded at the guard captain. "And don't worry about the boy. I've seen what he can do and who he is," he stated with confidence. "And between you and me, he may be one who helps to restore the order to a place of respect all over the realms."

CHAPTER FOURTEEN

Devol's home was rather quaint. It stood a couple of stories high on the outskirts of the city center. An effusion of flowers and simple paintings decorated the entrance and complemented the white, red, and pink cobblestone structure that had large windows on both floors. The aroma of something laced with honey cooking permeated the home and made the group all realize they were suddenly surprisingly hungry despite eating breakfast little more than an hour before.

The young swordsman walked up to the red front door and knocked loudly. "Mother!" he shouted and knocked again. "Mother, Father—are you home?"

"Well, if they were sleeping they aren't now," Jazai muttered. He paused to examine one of the paintings of a cat sleeping under starlight. Asla studied it with him over his shoulder.

"Devol?" A calm voice answered and caught the attention of the group. "Devol!" The voice grew more excited and footsteps ran to the entrance. The door was thrown open and a woman in a light blue dress stood in the aperture, relief and adoration on her face. "It is you."

"It is indeed," the boy replied cheerfully as they embraced. The spontaneous and genuine affection warmed the hearts of his companions. When they separated, he pointed to his team. "Mother, I would like to introduce you to some of the friends I've made in the Templars. This is Jazai, a scholar."

The diviner stepped forward and bowed. "It's a pleasure to meet you, ma'am."

"This is my friend Asla. She's one of the fastest magi I've ever seen," he announced and Asla's ear twitched as she also bowed to her.

"It is nice to meet you. I hope we aren't intruding."

"Oh, not at all!" Devol's mom assured her and extended a hand to the young wildkin so she would raise her head. "You are so adorable. Please feel welcome."

"Thank you kindly," Asla said and a small blush tinted her cheeks.

"And this"—Devol pointed to Wulfsun with a flourish—"is the man who has been helping me train, Captain Wulfsun."

"A captain! It's a pleasure to meet you. I am Lilli Alouest." She beamed and bowed to the elder Templar. "My husband is also a captain of the guard here in Monleans."

"So I've heard. Your son has told us all about you," Wulfsun replied. "I'm sorry to drop in like this, but we're on a mission that takes us through the city and we wanted to give Devol an opportunity to come and see you."

"Of course! It's no trouble. I am baking for the week so there's more than enough food to go around. Come on in."

The group followed her inside. The floors were a warm brown wood and she ushered them to a large rectangular table, where each took a seat. "Victor, come down! We have company," she called up the stairs before she walked to the kitchen.

"We do? Who has come?" a strong voice asked as footsteps descended the stairs. Devol's father entered the room in a white shirt and black trousers. His head was shaved clean but he had a large brown beard and thick eyebrows. His green gaze darted to the table and settled on the young swordsman, who waved at him with a smile.

Victor returned the smile, walked closer, and clasped the boy's hand to pull him into a hug. "It's good to see you, son." He ended the embrace as he looked at the others. "Are these all your Templar friends?"

"A few. I have more back at the order," the boy told him and pointed at each one as he ran through the list. "Asla, Jazai, and Captain Wulfsun. That's the abridged version. I've introduced them three times now."

"Three?" his father inquired as his mother entered with a basket of honey-drizzled bread and an assortment of cheeses.

"We ran into Castiel in the market," Devol explained as he broke one long loaf and passed it to the others. "We're on a mission but I wanted to come and see you before we continue to Levirei."

"A mission?" Victor asked as walked to a cabinet, selected a bottle of wine, and took a jug of fruit juice out of the cooling box. He placed these on the table, passed cups around, and uncorked the bottle before he offered some to

Wulfsun, who accepted with an enthusiastic nod. Devol poured juice for Asla, Jazai, and himself.

"Yeah. We're going to look into some disturbances in the area. It won't be a problem," he added reassuringly. Jazai noted that he seemed to skirt around the issue rather tactfully. "Hey, since I'm here, let me tell you more details of what we've been doing together for the last few months."

The young swordsman began to tell his parents selected stories of his time in the order—the training, meeting new realmers, and snippets of missions and quests that wouldn't alarm them too much. His companions began to feel more comfortable and added their recollections and tales. The table was now full of honeyed bread, fruits, cheeses, and slices of thin meats and they spent a couple of hours simply talking and getting to know one another.

Jazai delighted in telling odd stories and amusing mishaps in the Templar Order hall while Victor regaled them with similarly silly stories from the guardsmen. Lilli and Asla spoke of the mana arts and Asla told tales of wildkin lore and her people's history. Wulfsun and Victor shared war stories and memorable battles and both quickly earned the respect of the other.

Devol used this time to tell his friends more stories of his youth and his father's exploits as a guard captain and Jazai did the same of his father's travels. It was not until he unfastened his sword and placed it against the table and the ethereal glow seeped through the covering cloth that there was a sudden shift in his father's jovial demeanor.

"So, Devol," he began cautiously, rested his arms on the table, and pointed at the sword, "were you able to find out much about that blade during your stay with the Templars?"

"Hmm?" The boy swallowed a mouthful of cheese before he nodded. "Oh, right. I guess I never mentioned that in the letters."

"Are you serious?" Jazai muttered as he was about to take a bite of an apple. "I would have thought that would be one of the first things you told them about."

"I guess I was still getting used to it. It's not like I could tell them more than what I knew, which wasn't much," Devol pointed out with a shrug and looked at his mother. "But your hunch was right, mother. It is a majestic."

Lilli's joyful face fell somewhat and he recognized the look from the day in the Emerald Forest when the sword had first appeared. She nodded. "That's good to know, Devol, but...it was more than a hunch."

"What?" He looked at her in confusion. Victor and Wulfsun shared a look of silent communication and the Templar nodded. Devon's father returned the nod and sighed in response.

"So you didn't tell him?" he asked the other man.

Wulfson shook his head as he leaned back in his chair. "It didn't seem like our place to do so."

The parents nodded and looked briefly at each other before they bowed to the Templar captain. "That was thoughtful, thank you," Lilli said quietly and took the boy's hand. "It should probably come from us."

Everyone felt the mood shift immediately. Both of Devol's parents seemed rather tense and Victor gathered himself before he sighed heavily and looked him in his eyes

"Son, we should have been... We were aware of what the sword was. And we knew why it appeared to you."

"You did?" he asked, not so much shocked as curious. "Then why didn't you tell me right away?"

"We were hoping he would return to claim it since it..." Lilli began but her words faltered. "That majestic is tied to you because it is half of the majestic known as Achroma."

"Achroma?" Devol looked at the sword. "So it does have a name."

"It does, together with a long, many-storied history," his father added. "One that is still being written. As your mother said, that blade is tied to you, Devol, because your father tied it to you."

The young swordsman looked at him, his expression blank as he observed Victor, whose eyes misted slightly along with Lilli's. "Devol...the man who holds the other half of that sword is your real father. We...we are your guardians, not your parents."

Jazai and Asla shifted uncomfortably and glanced at their friend. His parents and Wulfsun kept their gazes fixed on him and awaited his reaction to the beginnings of the truth. Would it be sorrow, utter shock, or anger? None of these came, at least immediately.

Instead, Devol nodded, stretched with his other hand, and took a piece of white and orange cheese. He looked at it for a moment before he took a small bite as he simply nodded. "Yeah, I knew that."

CHAPTER FIFTEEN

The shocked and confused reaction did eventually come but from everyone except Devol. "Wait—what?" Victor gasped, now out of his chair "You knew?"

"Well, I had a good idea anyway, probably around the... ow, Mom! Your nails are digging into my hand," he cried. His mother was shaking with what seemed to be a mixture of sadness, relief, and a trace of terrifying anger.

"You knew?" she demanded. The shimmering magenta of her mana began to flare and the group noticed that several objects now hovered above the table. Most concerning were the pointy ones. "And you didn't say anything?"

"For a while, it was only a theory," Devol explained in hopes of calming her but it didn't help much. "It was when we were cleaning the house a couple of years ago during the dawning moon, remember?"

"Calm yourself, Lilli," Victor interjected. "Let the boy say his piece before you kill him."

"More assistance, Father, more," Devol demanded and finally wrenched his hand free. "I wasn't trying to string you along but as I grew up, I began to notice things."

"Like what?" Lilli asked and folded her arms as she stared at her son through long strands of hair.

"Well...first, we didn't look that much alike," he began and pointed at his face. "We share a couple of things like nose and face shape, but my auburn hair, my silver eyes... neither of you have either of those."

"They could simply have been recessive traits," Jazai pointed out and Devol looked at him with honest anger.

"Would you hold off for a while, please?" he asked and turned to the adults. "But that time when we cleaned and I was going through crates in the attic, I found an old book —a journal or something—and inside was a picture."

"A picture?" his mother asked and her mana paused enough that the objects fell slowly onto the table. "What picture, Devol?"

He took a deep breath and relaxed slightly. "Here, I'll go and find it." He stood quickly and dashed up the stairs, leaving the rest to look awkwardly at one another.

"I am...sorry for that outburst," Lilli apologized and straightened her hair. "I usually have better mana control than that."

"Ah, no need to worry," Wulfsun stated with a casual wave.

"You have impressive vello control, all things considered," Jazai remarked and finally bit into the apple as Asla glared at him. A few thumps issued from above before Devol raced down the stairs holding a dusty red book and an old photograph.

"Here—it was this one." He placed the photo in front of his parents. His father picked it up and stared at it with his mother. The photo was faded but the people in it could still be seen. One was a tall man with long auburn hair who wore a dark cloak and slacks with a weapon wrapped in a silk cloth on his back. The other was a woman with silver eyes and golden hair, who held a small child with a small patch of dark-red hair similar to the man's.

"This is..." Victor whispered and looked at the book on the desk. "This must have been left by Elijah before he left."

"I didn't realize this was here." Lilli sighed, took the photo, and looked mournfully at the woman. "Joche."

"When I saw those two in the photo, I realized I looked like both of them," Devol said quietly and folded his arms. "I didn't start out thinking they might be...the ones who bore me. Not until later." He looked at the sword. "Then, when everything happened with the majestic—Achroma—and dad mentioned his Templar 'friend,' it put another piece into place. After that, when I was on the journey to the Templar Order and everyone freaked out when they saw me, the sword, and the insignia on the map—"

"Wait, boy, you knew?" Wulfsun asked and leaned forward.

"You don't have the greatest poker faces," he stated with a shrug. "Vaust and Nauru made me think they knew whoever had the map, but you and the others were a little too obvious."

The Templar captain sighed in irritation and ran a hand through his hair. "You noticed that, eh? I thought you were a wee too wide-eyed to pay it much mind."

Jazai leaned closer to Asla. "Between this and last night, I'm beginning to wonder if it is only a ruse on his part."

She frowned but responded with a half-shrug. "I think you may not be completely wrong in this case."

"Did you have to add that last part?" The diviner sighed and took another bite of the apple.

Victor looked at his son. "Devol, even if you were only suspicious, why did you never bring it up?"

Devol stared at him for a moment, honestly baffled by the question as if that had never occurred to him. "Does it matter?" he replied and all gazes settled on him again. "As far as the majestic is concerned, sure, but my 'real' father? He isn't that to me." He walked around to take a seat in front of Victor and Lilli. "Not to be ungrateful to them"—he gestured to the picture—"but even if I did know they were my birth parents, they aren't the ones who raised me. You are."

His father's jaw clenched and his mother formed a smile, even with tears in her eyes. She wrapped him suddenly in her arms and he reciprocated after a moment of surprise. "Like I could think otherwise."

Jazai and Asla smiled and when they heard a sniffle behind them, they turned to see Wulfsun wiping his eye. "You are a softy under all that armor, eh?" the diviner teased.

"Can it," the man ordered gruffly, folded his arms, and stuck his chest out.

Devol chuckled as he looked at the Templar and then at his parents. "With that out of the way, there was something I wanted to ask you." His mother leaned back to look at him. "I've been training with Wulfsun and others in the order but he was rather insistent that I get permission from the two of you before he took me on as an apprentice. I wondered if we could talk about that now."

Victor drew a deep breath and nodded. "I see you've made your choice then?" he asked.

The boy thought about it before he nodded softly. "I know it's happened fast, but I do feel I can do more with the Templars and they have been good to me. I want to return that."

Lilli shook her head and giggled between her tearful sniffs. "To think I was worried about you joining the guards," she whispered and glanced at her husband. "What do you think?"

Victor looked at Wulfsun, then at Devol. "It's not unheard of for magi as young as you to set off on your own, but I wish we'd had more warning," he admitted and his gaze drifted to the picture. "Elijah did what he thought was best. He wanted you to have a real chance at a traditional life but you fell into this anyway. Even with Achroma bound to you, you had to call out to it first." He nodded and grasped his son's hand. "This is your call to answer, son. If you wish to walk this path, we will support you however we can."

Devol nodded, tightened his grip around his father's hand, and looked at Lilli. "Mother?"

She simply nodded and although her tears still fell, she gave him a silent blessing, the most she could give at that moment.

Wulfsun stood, walked closer, and placed a hand on the

boy's back. "I promise to look after him and we have a portal near the city. He can visit any time he wishes to."

"Thank you," Victor stated. The Templar nodded and left the family, taking Jazai and Asla outside for a spell to allow mother, father, and son to have a moment to themselves.

CHAPTER SIXTEEN

The group spent the night at the Alouest abode. The following morning, after a feast of a breakfast, they set out to one of the prides of Monleans, the Renaissance Central Station. Even though they arrived fairly early in the morning, the station was already bustling. Whistles and orders rang out as adventurers, merchants, travelers, and many others hastily found their routes and the right places to await their trains.

Devol looked at the black-and-gold archways that decorated the main concourse. Several train lines were huddled under the main building which had orange glass covering the ceiling that bathed the area in a sunny glow.

"This is one of our city's masterpieces," Victor said with pride. He was now dressed in the white-and-gold armor of the city guard, and on both hips were large curved blades with a grip in the middle that connected Glaives, his unique exotic. "Only Britana has more travel than Renaissance, but we still have the most elegant station in all the kingdoms."

"Monleans had the first cobalt grid trains as I understand," Wulfsun remarked as he looked around the station. The Templar stood head and shoulders above all others there.

"Indeed. They started to bring them in twelve years ago and most of the cobalt furnace trains have been phased out already," Victor added, so boastful one would think he had a hand in inventing them.

"Here, Devol, take these." Lilli insisted and handed her son two large bags. "The blue one has extra food for the trip," she explained. "And the white one has clothes and other supplies for when you return to the order hall."

"I'll be back, Mom, I promise!" he assured her and gave her another hug. "Like Wulfsun said, I'm only a portal away now."

"Is that our train?" Asla asked and pointed to one of the tracks. The group turned as a large, sleek train pulled into the station. It was white with gold trimming and white light streamed from under it as the mana transferred from the cobalt engine in the train and connected it to the tracks.

There were no doors on the front. Instead, a man in a white suit and hat teleported out and held a hand up as blue mana formed the word *Levirei* in the air. "Train to Levirei! All aboard!" he shouted and finished his declaration with a whistle as he began to march down the line. The group all began to hurry forward along with dozens of others.

Devol produced his ticket and an official punched it to allow him onto the transit area. The others did the same except for his parents, but thanks to his father's position, the man simply bowed and let them through to see their son off.

He loaded his bags onto a cart, which was taken by a bellhop whom he thanked with a few cobalt bits. As the cart was pushed away, he noticed a set of odd figures in the distance. There were four of them and all wore dark robes that shadowed their faces. They were dressed from head to foot in black, but he noticed an odd curve to the fingers of their gloves and felt a strange yet familiar presence from them. As he began to send mana into his eyes, a hurrying merchant bumped into him and almost knocked them both over.

"So sorry...not paying attention!" the man apologized and helped to stabilize him. "It's best to get on soon, young one. The train waits for no one." He stepped quickly on board and when the boy turned to look at the figures again, they were gone.

"Last call for Levirei!" the conductor shouted as he passed through on his way to the front of the train. He teleported inside once he reached his mark.

"We'd best get going," Wulfsun said and Devol turned to confirm that everyone was behind him. "Are the bags on board?"

He nodded absently. Although he wanted to mention the cloaked figures, he did not know where they had gone and he decided he shouldn't worry his parents at this juncture. He gave his mom one last hug and shook his father's hand as he and the others climbed aboard. Their train car was decorated with white carpet and similar orange glass above, which bathed the car in the same warm glow as the station. He found his seat, lowered the window, and waved to his parents as the train started. The car lifted slightly and he ducked inside before it set off and he closed the window.

"So, are you excited, apprentice?" Wulfsun chortled as he chose a seat across from the three and his bulk almost filled the row.

"Are you already calling me that?" Devol responded and folded his arms. "So you've finally come around, eh?"

The Templar stroked his beard and regarded him with an unrepentant look. "I never minded the idea at all. I merely wanted to make sure my ass was covered," he admitted and looked out the window as the fields of Renaissance flew past. "In case Elijah does come back, it's better to be safe."

The boy frowned as he thought about that. "So, Elijah… you make him sound like a rather stern man."

Wulfsun hesitated for a moment before he shrugged. "He's not exactly the rowdy type at all, but he is a gentle soul normally. It's merely best to not annoy him." He waved a large hand as if to dismiss the thoughts out of the air. "That's something you should still talk about with your parents. For now, I'll mark this as the official start of your apprenticeship. You'd best be prepared."

"Technically, you have been training him until now," Asla pointed out. "This is only…ceremonial, is it not?"

"Templars are big on ceremony." Jazai chuckled. "Haven't you noticed?"

Devol took a moment to look down the car from his seat. A stewardess was checking on passengers but he did not see any signs of the figures he'd noticed before.

"Is something wrong, lad?" Wulfsun asked, an eyebrow

raised as he looked curiously at the boy. "You seem anxious."

Devol wondered whether he should bother or not. Perhaps he was being paranoid. Before he could make his mind up, the Templar leaned forward. "Being your mentor is more than only training, Devol. If you need something, let me know."

The man's seriousness was rather disarming and he put his thoughts together quickly. "A few minutes before we left, I saw these guys—four of them—in dark robes. I couldn't shake the feeling that there was something off about them."

"Oh, good. It wasn't only me then." Jazai sighed. "I think they may have been dark magi. It's not technically illegal as long as they don't use blood magic or necromancy, but it's not exactly looked on favorably either."

"Pot and kettle," Wulfsun said as he stood. "I need to hit the head. If I run into them, I'll let you know. Or if you see them again, let me know."

"Understood," Devol confirmed with a nod.

"And start planning for when we get into the city," the Templar ordered as he slid out of his row. "When we get our boots on the ground, we need to be ready." With that, he left them and the train car and moved to the next one.

"Planning?" the young swordsman asked in bemusement and looked at the others.

Asla was equally as puzzled. "I'm not sure what we can accomplish. He's the one with all the plans."

"He's probably trying to sound like a general or something," Jazai quipped as he stretched his arms before he slid them behind his head to rest. "Welcome to being official Templar recruits."

Wulfsun walked casually through another train car and passed one of the restrooms. He had also caught a glimpse of the figures Devol had seen, and his anima was always up. They were more than odd. There was something foul about them. He knew they were aboard because he could feel them although he couldn't place them. The farther he moved down the train, the more he could sense them, and the lingering unease strengthened to a sickening aura.

He let a steward pass and both men gave the other a friendly nod. As soon as the official had left, he tried to open the door to the next train car but it was locked. He used a trickle of vis to force it open and grunted when the lock cracked loudly. Quickly, he stepped through and shut the door. This car was larger than the others—storage, most likely. He took a few more steps and could now feel the foul magic all around him. The interior was dark with only a few lights above and below to illuminate the space.

A rattle caught his attention a moment before something landed on the floor. Wulfsun strode forward and unleashed his anima as the cloaked figures emerged from the shadows. He stared intently at them but their hoods hid their faces. "Are you taking a walk there, lads?" he asked.

One of the cloaked figures held a hand up. A tattooed rune on the palm lit up and he braced for an attack.

Instead, the rune created a thin field around the car and everything immediately grew quiet.

"A silence spell?" he asked and thumped his fists together. "So it'll be an exciting walk, will it?" The cloaked figures let their gloves slip off to reveal gray, spotted skin and pointed nails. Two of them brandished jagged daggers.

"Oh, I see." Wulfsun grinned and punched his fists together until the knuckles cracked. "Quite exciting, then?"

CHAPTER SEVENTEEN

The strangers attacked first. Those with only their claws lunged at the Templar and swung the talons down as Wulfsun raised his gauntlets to block them. A blast released as his majestic activated to coat his body in a hardened mana shield. The barrier knocked them back and slowed the strikes of the other attackers.

The Templar moved to the side. He had little room in the car to maneuver but enough to let their attack slide past as he powered his fist into the back of one man's head and hurled him into the assailant behind him. The other attempted to strike at his throat and he noticed a coating of liquid running down the blade—poison, no doubt.

He was able to snatch the figure by the wrist. At least they appeared to be smart enough to aim for the places that weren't armored, but as he wrestled with the dagger-wielding attacker, he was finally able to shake its hood off. He recoiled instinctively when he understood why they had such a sickening presence.

The assassin's skin was gray and his eyes were lifeless

with nothing but yellowed corneas and no irises. It had the appearance of a male but had been shaven bald and brow-less and its mouth was sewn shut. A dark spot between its eyes allowed a small trickle of mana to seep out.

These were ghouls, corpses reanimated by magic and under someone's control. When the surprise wore off, the entity lifted a leg and drove it into Wulfsun's chest. Although it did no damage, the force was strong enough to jostle him and make him take a step back. This weakened his hold and allowed it to wrest its hand free. The Templar snarled as he tried to adjust to this new reality of ghouls that could use vis. It was unusual, even in this strange moment.

The being he had previously knocked back had begun to recover. It focused on the Templar's undefended back as its comrades began to descend on their quarry. One of them raised a hand that formed ice around the fingertips. Wulfsun could sense the ghoul behind him preparing to strike as the three others moved toward him.

He straightened and lifted a leg as the creature in front of him fired an ice lance and the assailant behind him prepared to stab its dagger into the back of his neck. When he slammed his foot down, it activated his great barrier around him. The ice lance struck it and broke apart, while the dagger met the barrier and shattered. He balled a fist, turned, and dropped the shield as he drove his fist into the chin of the ghoul behind him. The blow landed with a sick-ening crack and launched the being into the roof of the train car. Its skull was crushed by the impact with the metal and it fell heavily, and what little mana was left within evaporated.

"Yer master must have not known who he was dealin' with." Wulfsun snarled defiance, his voice almost a growl more akin to a beast than a man. He turned to face the remaining assassins. "Or perhaps I wasn't your primary target. You were after the kids." The gauntlet on his right hand began to glow with his yellow mana as he placed a hand atop his fist and held it firmly while he concentrated his mana and anger. "No matter. There's no use in keeping you alive when you can't even talk."

The ghouls seemed to realize their impending doom and launched themselves at the Templar in one last vain attempt to stop him. They only rushed to their second deaths. Wulfsun swung his powered fist into the face of the first one he could reach. The head exploded from the force of the punch but when the hit connected, the mana stored in the gauntlet was unleashed in a wave of force empowered by the mana.

It catapulted his three assailants across the car and shattered the doors holding the cargo along the sides so the contents spilled out. The ghouls had no control and the energy carried them like they were caught in the winds of a cyclone. Only when they slammed into the other end of the car and their forms broke against it did they finally stop.

They crumpled and the remnants of mana that maintained their bodies dispersed into the air before it vanished, along with the silencing cantrip surrounding the car. Wulfsun drew a breath and let his anima withdraw a little. He shook his head when he realized he'd let himself get too hot, which wasn't smart in any battle. They might have been assassins but even if their purpose was to try to kill the kids, they would not have made proper training dummies given their ineptness.

He turned to look at the first ghoul he'd eliminated, knelt beside it, and examined the hole in its head—or what remained of it. It must have been the connection point where the controller of the macabre minions stored their anima to give them life and bind them to them, but something seemed wrong. Like he had thought earlier, this master of theirs must have been either looking down on them or incompetent.

They needed to be close to have proper control of the ghouls without sacrificing power, and given all the oddities of the beings like using cantrips and vis, he had to deduce that these weren't the ordinary shambling bodies he was more accustomed to. As such, they needed a more powerful connection than normal. The train car rattled slightly. Unless their controller was able to keep up with the vehicle, sending them on board was a poor decision.

He closed his eyes and felt for mana in the air but discerned nothing unusual. In fact, he and the three young ones seemed to be the most powerful beings aboard at the moment, which meant it was unlikely the controller was on the train themselves. He could have deduced that without much thought. Vello was not his specialty like Vaust and Freki but someone controlling ghouls like this would have stood out to him.

His thumb dug into something and he opened his eyes and recoiled when the ghoul began to soften. Black liquid seeped from its body as it turned to mush. Without the mana to keep its form together and the rigors it went through, it was now dissolving in his hands. He looked at the others but they had yet to start decomposing, although he had no doubt they would soon follow.

Wulfsun looked around hastily. He had to get rid of them. There was no need to cause an incident as the staff would probably already have issues to deal with when they returned to this train car. He noticed a hatch above, grasped the ladder on the side, and lowered it before he took hold of the ghoul's robes and dragged it with him. Quickly, he scrambled up, undid the latch, and pushed the hatch open. He poked his head out.

They were passing through a forest now, which provided sufficient cover. He manhandled the body through and hurled it out into the trees as hard as he could, hoping no one in any of the cars behind could see as they drove past. Working quickly, he dragged the other bodies up one at a time and disposed of them in the same way. Although he was relieved to be rid of them, he was somewhat annoyed that he had to throw potential leads away.

He shut the hatch and replaced the ladder. With a sigh, he stroked his beard and he surveyed the car around him and all the luggage that had fallen during the fight. Among the wreckage, he found one of the daggers but the dark sludge had consumed it and melted it like the ghouls. He covered his gauntlet in mana and crushed what remained of the blade. There should have been another one somewhere there but he couldn't locate it in the limited time at his disposal.

With a baleful glance at the luggage scattered around the car, he sighed. He certainly did not have the time to try to make this right. They would be pulling into Levirei in about twenty to thirty minutes. Reluctantly, he turned to the door and checked to see if anyone in the next car had noticed him before he stepped through. It would be best to get back to the others and let them know there might be a slight delay in getting their possessions once they reached the city.

CHAPTER EIGHTEEN

As the train raced past the Arkalod Mountains, now only ten minutes from its destination, a figure in a dark cloak and cowl grimaced and shattered the mirror in his hands that he had used to watch his slaves fail. Salvo composed himself, dusted the shards from his gloves, and made sure none had pierced his hand. He sighed and wandered into the cave as he acknowledged that he'd been too eager and sent the ghouls in too early.

If he had waited, perhaps the Templar would have returned to his car rather than proceed farther. Or maybe he should positioned them around an occupied car that might have at least given him pause. Then again, this one seemed more feral than the mori so he might not have minded the collateral damage.

He stopped a few steps into the cave and glanced at the three remaining ghouls still seated motionlessly on the floor where he had left them. Thoroughly disgruntled, he leaned against the wall and considered what he should do next now that his plan had failed. A thought occurred to him, one that should have been easy to answer but now eluded him. What was the point of the preemptive attack in the first place?

Would he have been satisfied if the ghouls had killed the brats? In all honesty, he would not mind if the Templar was dead, but that could have caused complications. Perhaps the others would have given up on the mission if their leader had been killed. That would have ruined everything.

So why had he done it? He felt there was something important—some kind of edge he had overlooked. Perhaps it was not to kill the Templars but to observe them? That sounded right. After all, it was not knowing about the Templars' powers that almost cost him last time, so why did it escape him? He slid his hand to the box attached to his waist and tapped it absently. Was it already getting to him?

Salvo shook his head and sighed, walked out of the cave, and observed the sky. What did it matter if the plan failed? This would be better. All that tricky, subterfuge crap was Koli's specialty and why did he try to do this like Koli? This was his mission and he would do it like he wanted to do it.

He looked at the tracks. The train would pull into the city any moment now. There wasn't much chance that he could reach them and strike while they were sightseeing. It would probably cause satisfying chaos, but Levirei's guards were no joke and there were at least a dozen guilds in the city. He wouldn't last long, even if he abandoned the ghouls. Dammit, he might have made the attempt if he had a team of the big ones, but he was left with the freaks' scraps.

His gaze was drawn away from the city to the east, where in the distance, he could faintly see a dark patch of sky, something strange enough to make someone suspicious. That was where they would eventually go and it seemed the best place to intercept them or at least catch up. The ghouls weren't as fast as he was and a part of him knew he would want to be prepared this time, even if he would not admit that to anyone.

When he snapped his fingers, his undead servants stood as one and stalked behind him as he ran a hand over the dark box. The contents hummed and he could hear it growl, wanting release. This time, he would be prepared and nothing they could do would prepare them for it.

"Arriving in Levirei!" a conductor announced over the box speakers in the cars. "Also, it appears there was a mishap in one of the luggage cars. We are quickly righting this oddity but there may be a slight delay. Our deepest apologies."

"Did you hear that, Wulfsun?" Jazai chuckled and stretched as the train slowed. "You bumbling around the luggage knocked their schedule off a little. It's not very professional."

Devol shifted in his seat and glanced at the diviner with what he hoped was sufficient warning for him to keep it down "You still haven't told us what happened when you left."

The large Templar shrugged. "I told you. I went looking

for the guys in robes, found them, and took care of them. What more do you need?"

"Well, you could have told us that was your plan," the boy remarked as the train came to a complete stop. "From what you told us, we could have dealt with them."

"I didn't know that at the time." The man pushed to his feet as the doors to the train car opened. "Besides, it would have looked more suspicious with all of us walking around."

"At least we would have had something to do," Jazai muttered and straightened his jacket as he and the others stood to follow. "Seriously, what kind of line was that? Planning for when we get to the city? You have all the plans."

"We could have at least helped to clean the mess you made," Asla added.

"You're gonna keep harpin' on that, are ye?" Wulfsun sighed, ducked through the smaller doorway so he could debark, and stretched his arms with a yawn. "I cleaned up something far more disgusting than they would want to deal with. It's even, now go and wait for the bags and meet me at the exit."

Devol and Asla nodded and moved to the luggage cart while Jazai shook his head and followed. The first action on the trip and they didn't see any of it, the diviner thought morosely. When they reached the cart, the young swordsman handed one of the attendants a ticket and they searched for their bags. Asla tugged on his shirt and pointed to two conductors examining something that looked like a dagger.

The three wandered closer and Asla asked what they

were doing with her dagger, which successfully confused them. Her two companions remained relaxed with neutral expressions as she explained that it was an heirloom she valued too much to ever leave home without it in her possession, although she hardly ever used it. The conductors apologized, handed it to her, and surmised that it must have fallen out of her luggage when everything collapsed. They added that she needed to keep it hidden while in the city as it could cause problems with the local guard.

She agreed and thanked them and the group remained silent as the two men walked away to prepare the train. When they were far enough away to not notice, the three friends studied the dagger. "It looks like the ones Wulfsun said they attacked with," Devol pointed out.

"Hopefully, it is. If not, we stole someone else's," Jazai responded and ran his hand over the handle. "It's enchanted, but not an exotic. The spell makes it more durable and it loses its edge at a slower rate."

Asla lifted it to her nose, sniffed it, and gasped. She moved it away and wafted a hand around her nose. "It's poisoned, although little remains. My nose tells me it's a mixture of black caps, vantalace, and death root."

"That last one is no surprise." Devol folded his arms. "I'm not sure if there is a fatal poison that doesn't use at least a little death root."

"Most top-graded assassin recipes call for it but it doesn't make it plentiful, though," Jazai commented and looked at Asla. "Liquid or powder?"

"Liquid. There isn't enough residue for it to be powder, and it left..." She looked around, picked up a small pebble, and rubbed the blade to bring up a dark, inky gunk webbing. "Grime?"

"Baggage 1S!" an attendant called and startled Devol.

"That is us. I'll be right back!" he stated as he jogged to the cart. "Head to Wulfsun. I'll catch up!"

"Got it!" Jazai shouted as he and Asla began to head out of the station. She held the dagger by the handle, careful to avoid the blade. "Illusion," he whispered and distorted the weapon to look like a wand-shaped curio. "It won't last long but we won't be stopped unless someone is watching us closely."

She nodded and slid it under her shawl. "That might be a possibility given that assassins were sent after us."

The diviner shrugged. "Agreed, but hey, that means we're making our way in the world now, right? People have to care if they are trying to kill us."

The wildkin frowned but a small chuckle escaped as they proceeded through the crowd. "That might be the most optimistic interpretation I've ever heard you put on something."

"It's nice to potentially have fans out there, right?" Jazai quipped with a devious smirk. "I only hope we get to meet them soon. I'd like to return the favor."

CHAPTER NINETEEN

"Oy, over here!" Wulfsun shouted to Jazai and Asla from the western archway. "I'm glad to see you finally. Where's Devol?"

The diviner pointed to the train. "He offered to get the luggage. While we were waiting, we found this." Asla brought the knife out, still camouflaged as the curio.

"A wand." The Templar looked at them in confusion. "Are you collecting souvenirs or something?"

Jazai chuckled, then muttered, "It seems simple tricks can work on veterans as well."

"Touch it," Asla said and held it up handle-first so he wouldn't brush against the blade. The Templar touched the wand and frowned. "Metal—is this one of those knives?"

"Most likely. A couple of the conductors found it in the luggage area," Jazai explained and motioned for the Templar to lower the item. "I'll release the illusion but keep it out of sight." He snapped his fingers and the illusion dropped and the wand transformed into the jagged blade.

Wulfsun nodded as soon as he had examined it. "No

doubt about it, this is one of the daggers those ghouls had on 'em." He frowned and resisted the urge to run a finger over the blade. "I should have made sure I tossed them all out, but the other one disappeared inside the goop."

"I'm not sure if it tells us much." Asla sighed. "It doesn't appear unique enough to give us any indication of what it could have been made of. Jazai said it was enchanted, I suppose for durability or sharpness, and the poison coating it is made of black caps, vantalace, and death root."

Even though his hands were protected by his gauntlets, Wulfsun flinched and made a disgusted face. "That's the mixture for basilisk venom. It causes your body to freeze before it eventually shuts down—nasty stuff." He took out one of the small pouches on his belt, opened it, and slid the knife in, although the hilt still protruded a little. "Maybe our correspondent can tell us about anyone who might have targeted the client and gotten us mixed up in this. Otherwise, it seems the most likely reason behind this is these were assassins sent by those who created the disturbance we're investigating."

"I'll go with the second idea," Jazai said quietly. "If someone wanted to kill the count or lord or whoever hired us, there's no reason to include us unless they are simply spiteful."

"I still don't see how they would know who we are," Asla continued. "I would imagine the client received our details several hours ago. It seems too short a short a time to discover our mission, make a plan, and find people to try to assassinate us—unless they were expecting the Templars to send someone."

"Well, if they are using ghouls, they probably have

enough bodies," Wulfsun reasoned before he sighed and shook his head. "Sorry. That wasn't meant to be a pun or anything like that."

Jazai shrugged again and tapped his foot. "What the hells is taking Devol so long?"

"I'm here!" the swordsman shouted and followed it with a grunt of effort. They all looked to where the boy struggled with several different bags and satchels. They dangled from his back and arms and a smaller one was even slung across his neck. "I forgot how much we brought."

"You can push those two heavy doors in the order hall open but can't manage a few bags?" Jazai teased.

"It's not the weight. They are awkward to carry," Devol explained with a faint frown. "Do you want to try to carry all of this?"

"Yeah, sure." The diviner waved a hand and all the bags glowed with a faint blue light. All but Devol's bags elevated off him and moved to their respective owners.

The swordsman's frown deepened. "Show off," he mumbled and tightened his pack. "Next time, you're the bag carrier."

"It's probably wise," the other boy remarked with a smug grin and glanced at their leader. "Are we off now?"

"Aye, to the Red Wolves Den," Wulfsun stated. "It's a tavern in the city where we are meeting our contact."

"The lord?" Devol asked.

The Templar shook his head. "One of his bodyguards or something is gonna meet us and give us a briefing before we head to the boss. It's a safety procedure."

"Do they think the Templar would reason to threaten his life?" Asla asked as the group began to walk down the large flight of stairs to the bottom of the station and onto the road to the interior of the city.

"Nah. Many may not be thrilled with us but I don't think most believe us to be malicious, merely fools at worst," Wulfsun stated. "Not this fellow, though. Still, people in his position can be paranoid. It could be there are some who have targeted him and he merely wants to cover his bases."

"How will we recognize the contact?" Devol asked.

The Templar felt in one of his satchels and retrieved a golden coin with the Templar insignia. "She's holding a table for us in a private room. When we arrive, we show her this coin to prove we are the Templars her lord sent for."

The boy nodded and shifted his gaze to take in the sight of Levirei. It was not the size of Monleans but it was still a large, beautiful city. The central spires of the council building gleamed under the sunlight and the sun inched closer to the mountains in the distance. It would be dark soon and by that time, they might be in battle. He placed a hand on the hilt of his majestic. Even if he had an idea of what they were going against, they still had no real clue where it came from and what it was. That would not change his mind now, but as they drew closer to facing it, anxious anticipation began to gnaw at him.

Wulfsun opened the door to the Red Wolves Den, where they were greeted by the sight of large tables around which tradesmen, adventurers, and guards drank and dined, talking amongst each other. Lit dark metal chandeliers swung above. The group was dressed and armed better than most of the patrons there and so turned a few heads, but the one who drew most of the attention was the giant armored Templar who strode through, looking around for assistance.

"Welcome to Red Wolves," a barkeep shouted they turned to approach him. "What can I get you, sir? No alcohol for the young ones."

"Well, there goes my evening," Jazai quipped quietly and drew a chuckle from Devol.

Wulfsun leaned over the bar and his large arms almost slid off. "I'm looking for...Farah Malik. She should have a private room waiting for us."

The man nodded and beckoned to a hovering waitress. "Indeed. She got here a while ago. Follow Abby. She'll take you to the room."

"This way, sir," the short, blonde woman called to them over the loud conversations. Wulfsun nodded and gestured for the others to follow. They ascended the stairs of the tavern and walked into a short hall, where two guards stood watch and turned their heads to look at them.

"Good evening. This group is here for Ms. Malik." Abby said and motioned to the team.

"Identification?" one of the guards asked coldly as he turned fully toward them to block their path. Wulfsun produced the coin and handed it to him. He checked it carefully, then nodded at his comrade and Wulfsun. "She's waiting inside. Thank you for arriving on such short notice."

"When weird things happen...well, it is our job to deal

with them." The Templar chuckled, took the coin, and placed it securely in his satchel. The other guard opened the door while the first one resumed his original position. They let them pass and enter the room.

The interior was rather sparse but cozy with a nicer round table than those below and a couple of paintings of Levirei hanging on the wall. On the table were plates of meat, cheeses, and fruits, a large container of ale, and two pitchers of different juices.

At the far side of the table sat a woman in a silver chest plate with a red silk shirt beneath. She had white hair bound in a small ponytail, her skin was tanned, and she had piercing hazel eyes with curved oil markings on the side. Her chin rested on her hands as she studied the group when they all walked in and took seats on the opposite side of the table.

"Farah Malik?" Wulfsun asked and placed a hand on his chest plate. "Baio Wulfsun. I'm one of the captains of the Templar Order." He raised a hand to gesture toward Devol and his friends. "These are my soldiers, Devol, Asla, and Jazai."

"They seem quite young to be Templars," Farah noted, her voice calm but frank. "Or to be handling a mission such as this."

"I have a feeling this will be a long discussion," Asla muttered quietly, almost to herself, but Devol caught it and nodded. He had the same feeling himself.

"They are young but they have proven themselves skilled enough to be here," Wulfsun replied, his tone firm. "Besides, what your lord is paying for is me."

The woman nodded. "I'll take you at your word,

Captain. I can see they all have majestics so they have to be skilled enough to wield those, at least."

"Do you have one?" Devol asked and looked curiously at her garb to see if anything stood out.

She shook her head, reached under the table, and produced a sword in a scabbard. "I do not but my exotic can stand up to any majestic."

"I'm sure it can," Jazai commented, reading his tome. He felt a glare from Asla and turned to look at her. "What? I'm serious. According to her memories, she has fought against majestics and won a couple of times too."

"Are you reading my mind?" Farah asked with a sly smirk. "I suppose I can't be too upset. This can be considered your way of checking me."

"That was the idea, yes," the diviner replied with a sly smirk.

"I've dealt with diviners before so if you have what you need, let me take a guess as to how to deal with that." She flared her anima. It was yellow, similar to Wulfson's but a few shades paler.

Jazai raised an eyebrow and looked at his tome, now reading only her current thoughts. His smirk disappeared as he pursed his lips at what he read, then looked at her. "Well, that is unnecessarily hurtful."

"But it is amusing." Asla snickered as she read the tome over his shoulder.

He moved the book away and scowled. "Would you mind your own business?"

"Ha-ha! I like her wit," Wulfsun declared, also reading the book as the boy had moved it close to him when he tried to get it away from the wildkin.

"Oh, come on now!" Jazai sighed and the Templar snatched the book from him.

"If you can serve it you should be able to take it, Jazai." The man chortled as he flipped the pages back. "Let's see here...ah, I was right." He pointed toward the guard. "You are Osiran."

"I am." She nodded and put her sword down. "And before you ask, yes I was born and raised there. I joined my lord's employ after I assisted in defeating a bandit raid during a visit. He offered me a better position and pay."

"Do you miss it?" Asla asked and her ears flattened slightly.

"Sometimes," she responded casually. "I prefer the temperature here. You grow accustomed to the dry climate in Osira but I was born in Rokati, which is more tropical. The food is better there as well. We prefer more varied spices than you do here in Renaissance."

"We had some of our order headed to Osira," Devol mentioned and a metal hand slapped the back of his head which made him hit the table. "Ah!"

"It's not the kind of thing you mention casually, boy!" Wulfsun folded his arms in disapproval. "Well, now that it's been mentioned, there has been a sighting of something similar to what you described in your homeland."

"I am aware of that," Farah revealed, which surprised him. "I stay in contact with some of my friends and associates in my clan. On top of that, these...irregularities are popping up all over. We have been in contact with other kingdoms and these dark spots have formed across the land. From what I know, there is the one here in Levirei, one in Osira near Yastan, and one in the kingdom of Kanako as well. Britana is probably the worst off. I've heard that there are two there. I assume there are others in Soel, Fredom, and Norvian as well but they have not informed us—or the capital hasn't, at least."

"I see," Wulfsun nodded. "Then we should probably get to work. If we can find a way to destroy or shut down these 'dark spots,' I want to return to tell my order so others can deal with them more efficiently."

"Understood and well spoken." She picked her sword up and pushed from her chair. "Take whatever you wish from the table. We'll go by carriage to the council towers where Lord Maximillian awaits."

"Maximillian?" Jazai asked and looked at his teammates. "Is that his last name?"

"No, it is his first," Farah said. "He prefers to use his first name and says it shows that he is simply another one of the people."

"But you still call him lord," Asla noted.

"Yes, he prefers that as well." Farah sighed and took a bite of one of the cheeses as she moved to the door. "I should give you fair warning, My lord is somewhat…eccentric."

"Of course he is," Wulfsun grumbled and snatched the flask of ale. "I know these types and am probably gonna need this. Let's go, you three."

CHAPTER TWENTY

"So you see, mister..." Lord Maximillian Torvel trailed off as a servant poured another glassful of wine into a freakishly large goblet.

"Wulfsun, your lordship." Wulfsun muttered something under his breath. He tried his best to remain calm and composed and made a good show of it. Devol intercepted irate glares from both Jazai and Asla at the casual demeanor of this lord. Given the circumstances, one would think he would be more earnest.

The man placed his feet on his desk and motioned to a chair in front of him. "Yes, my apologies. It's been such a busy last few days. I'm certainly glad you accepted the offer I posted on behalf of the city."

"On behalf of all the lords?" Devol asked. "I thought this was on behalf of the military or the city itself."

Maximillian raised an eyebrow in scorn. "Hmm... Oh yes, you are from Monleans. Everything runs through the king and his cabinet. You see, my dear boy, that is not how things are run here in Levirei. Although it is not your fault that you don't understand that." He leaned forward and slipped his hand inside the pocket of his jacket to retrieve a small box decorated in red and yellow and adorned with symbols that looked like a serpent swallowing its tail.

"My apologies," Devol said because it seemed like the right thing to do. He glanced at his friends. Asla merely shrugged and gave him a sorrowful look while Jazai stared out the window and wondered if the seven stories to the streets below were enough for him to successfully commit suicide. "In that case, can you tell us why you were the one to post the mission?"

"He's rather new to this, isn't he?" Maximillian asked as he took a rootstick from his ornate box and lit it. Violet smoke drifted slowly through the air. "It is fine, however. In fact, it is rather delightful to see one so young take up a cause and one born in our capital, no less. Did you know I'm running for lordship of economics next year when Sera Equio retires?"

"I hope it works out for you," Wulfsun replied with a small sigh. "But if we could get back to the matter of these anomalies—"

"Yes, yes, of course. Very well," Maximillian interrupted with a wave of his hand. "I shall repeat myself, if only because my request is so important to me and my legacy." He took another drag and sip from his vices. "Give me a moment. Every time I think about this travesty, I think I might lose my mind and die."

"I've learned I'm never that lucky," Jazai mumbled as he studied the rings on his fingers and peered at the number of guards in the room before he sighed and clasped his hands behind his back. "Please take all the time you need, even until the sun sets."

Maximillian scoffed. "That's not for another hour and a half."

"I'm sure he's aware of that." Devol forced himself to relax in the chair provided. He took a moment to study the aristocrat in front of him. Maximillian might have been insufferable as a person but as a lord, he fit the part with his long blond hair, light in color to the point of being white almost like Farah's, a high brow, sunken cheeks, and plucked, narrow eyebrows atop deep green eyes. The eyes had a rather obvious enchanting on them as they had a sparkling glow and the shade would slowly lighten to a pleasant green that reminded him of the trees of the Emerald Forest. They would then darken to a shadowy jungle-green. His best guess was that he used these for seduction and he wondered if he could ask if they worked at all and were good for the job.

He was dressed in a closed long jacket decorated like his rootstick box—a red body with golden trim and buttons. His slacks and heeled boots were both solid black. It was difficult to make out the material in the dim light but given the almost perfect fit and attention to the stitching, they must have cost more than the entirety of Devol's wardrobe and more.

"Well, thank you for the offer but I seem to have miraculously composed myself." The lord straightened and rested his hands on the desk.

"Oh, joy," Wulfsun muttered and took a quick drag of a cigar that one of the servants had offered and he'd originally refused. "So, what is the short version of the story?"

The lord took a drink from his glass and moved the bangs of his hair to uncover his face so he could stare bemusedly at the Templar.

"It would seem that some of my...associates have not been forthcoming about the current issues with regards to this dark spot near the city. In particular, how so many people have gone missing and the odd shadow creatures that constantly appear. Some of my personal guards and my more astute personnel have patrolled and studied the area. The lord of the military has increased the watch around the walls and sent a few more groups of troops to guard the area and cut down any of the monstrosities that crawl out, but even with the lady of academics bringing in scholars and magi to ward it, there is no sign that it might dissipate or anything."

He sighed dramatically. "At best, it seems to contain it to some extent. We've lost many good people, both in disappearances and those who have had some...mental difficulties in dealing with surveys into the area. Naturally, this is upsetting the populace. So what we decided to do is bring experts in from areas outside the city who have more...freedom to do what they wish."

The insinuation was not lost on Wulfsun but he ignored it. "You mean people like the Templars?"

"We considered a number of guilds and experts, but I believe you are one of the best suited for such things." Maximillion smiled wryly before he finished the last of his drink. "Normally, we would reach out to our guilds here in Levirei or perhaps in the capital. But given that this mess is spreading to other kingdoms and considering your unique skill set, I insisted that you be hired." He beckoned the servant with the wine bottle again and the man stepped forward and filled the goblet with the last of the contents of the bottle.

"And that is appreciated," Wulfsun stated and folded his arms. "So some of your people go missing and none of the usual tricks have worked in dealing with this anomaly. Calling the Templar isn't a bad course of action but I'm curious about something, Lord Maximillian. With what we know, I would guess this is shadow or blood magic of some kind. Wouldn't the better option be to contact a warlock guild? They deal with this type of problem as well and would probably be cheaper."

"Cheaper?" Jazai whispered to the others. "How much are they being paid for this. Do we get a cut?"

"It's a fair question," Devol replied.

"Not now, both of you," Asla stated and watched the lord suspiciously as they waited for his response.

"Mr. Wulfsun, I'm beginning to think you believe I have some kind of ulterior motive in hiring your order or potentially think of me as an idiot," Maximillian replied, although a small smile crept onto his face. The Templar tilted his head and waited for him to continue. "However, I am a gentleman and I will not lie so yes, I have my suspicions about what this is and believe the Templars are the best choice to deal with it." He took a long drag and let the smoke billow out as he spoke. "I hope you are not so cynical as to believe running an empire must take no more than charisma and expensive taste alone. So now that I know the general knowledge, let me interest you with a personal theory."

In the next moment, something happened that briefly

knocked the Templars out of their scornful attitude. The man's demeanor changed. It would not have seemed obvious to most but the small smile on his lips became a wider, eerie grin although his body language revealed next to nothing. Still, the haughty air of the lord seemed to vanish, his poise seemed cold, and his shifting eyes seemed to change reflexively to their darker shade.

"Because I find something rather interesting about this anomaly and potentially, there is much to gain from it as well." His nonchalant tone vanished and was replaced by a frosty tone, and the way he spoke made every word sound like liquid pouring from his mouth. Farah, who had stood silently beside him all this time, flinched slightly at his change in demeanor. "I believe this anomaly is exactly that —an anomaly or an enigma, something that shouldn't be and we don't yet truly understand." He finished his drink and placed the empty glass on the table. He settled his elbows on the desk, intertwined his fingers, and rested his chin on them. "You Templars, as an order, have more leniency than most. I wish to make use of that. From what I understand, you are rather knowledgeable about partic- ular items of...a cursed disposition."

Devol stared at him, surprised that he knew of malefics. And if he read him right, if he knew of malefics and what they could do, he seemed to want to use them.

"If I am right that something is channeling this power or even creating it, I would like to have it in my possession. I know that is not in the mission details themselves, but consider this a personal request to you. Should you be interested, I can pay you quite—"

"I can't promise anything," Wulfsun interrupted and his

gaze fixed icily on the lord. "I can't say I know what you are getting at, but if something is controlling this mess, it needs to be destroyed. Hells, from what I understand, that may be the only way to stop this anomaly, dark spot, or whatever the hells it is. We're here to do exactly that, not get you a new trinket."

The light from the office's windows dimmed as the sun fell slowly from the sky and cast a dusky light on the group. The lord frowned briefly but shrugged and leaned back. "I can certainly understand that. It's a pity, but I think it might have turned out to be a bother anyway." He looked at the group, noticed their majestics, and pointed them out. "Do you use them well?" he asked with a smirk.

"Yes," the Templar replied. "We will find out what this dark spot is and if we can stop it, we will."

Maximillian nodded and motioned to the woman beside him. "Farah shall accompany you. She is highly skilled in swordsmanship and the use of light magic. And, of course, if you feel the need to have backup, any of the guardsman wearing red-and-gold armbands are under my employ. Simply tell them to accompany you under my authority."

"Again we appreciate it, but that second part won't be necessary," Wulfsun stated and nodded at Farah. "Having light magic could be of use, though." She nodded in reply.

The lord leaned back in his chair and studied the group in a careless way. "Then I wish you the best of luck. If you accept this mission, take the carriage to the site. They already await you." He placed a hand over his heart. "Oh, and if you fail and sadly pass on from this world, I promise you a beautiful funeral." This earned mixed reactions in the room and Devol felt more ill around this lord than at the possibility of facing the anomaly.

"What a kind gesture," the Templar said gruffly, finished the cigar, and stamped it out as he stood "Consider this my acceptance and again, that last part won't be needed."

Maximillian raised his hands and clapped three times. A gray-haired, white-suited servant or perhaps bodyguard given his size entered the office quickly enough to indicate that he'd stood outside the door. He walked to Maximillian's side and produced a small book—a journal, it seemed —and handed it to Wulfsun, who began to flip through the pages. "Feel free to read that whenever you please. It contains a few notes, pictures, and the like of what we know so far. Do what you need to do but I do have a request." The Templar looked up from the book and raised an eyebrow. "If you do find yourself overwhelmed, try to make it to the main site alive. Even if you expire, we could probably learn much from the autopsy."

"Are you joking?" Jazai's growled tone was so low the man fortunately didn't hear him.

"We'll keep it in mind, your lordship." Their leader looked at the youngsters. "You know the stakes now. Do you still wish to continue?"

The three friends nodded and stood close together. Wulfsun began to walk out of the office and Devol turned to follow. "Oh, and you—the one from Monleans!" Maximillian called. The boy turned to see he still wore his chilly smile. "I hope I can have your vote next year. I hope to see you again."

He merely nodded and hurried to catch up to the others. Honestly, he hoped to never see this man again.

CHAPTER TWENTY-ONE

The cobalt-fueled carriage hovered only a few inches above the road. They had left the city of Levirei far behind them and the conveyance was taking them to the dark spot site. Their arrival was only several minutes away. Inside the carriage, the group examined the journal with the information Maximillian's employees had gathered thus far on the anomaly.

It provided minimal details, unfortunately. Almost anyone who ventured inside—even protected by exotics, enchanted gear, and wards—would either not return or came back mentally scarred. Their only communication seemed to be yells and scattered mumblings of darkness and monsters. When they had been healed or calmed, which usually took days, they could barely recall anything from within the ebon space they had ventured into.

Devol looked at one of the photos, supposedly a sighting of one of the creatures that had streamed out of the anomaly, but it merely looked like a black blob gliding above the grasslands of Levirei.

"Those are useless." Farah sighed. He looked at her and she offered him a sketch. "These creatures don't have a form unless you can see them using anima. We even tried using cameras with enchanted film and glass infused with traces of cobalt but it didn't help much and those pictures are the best we have. These sketches are slightly more accurate."

He put the picture down and took the sketch. Jazai and Asla looked over his shoulder. On the page was nothing more than a shadowy, human-shaped being with little white dots for eyes and no discernible features. "This was the best you could get?" the diviner asked.

"That's what they look like to most people," she explained. "At least that is how I've seen them when I've patrolled. They aren't particularly strong but they are tenacious and direct physical attacks don't do anything against them. We've had strong guards attack with all manner of weapons, but unless they use weapons enchanted with certain magics, like light, even if they do injure the creatures, they simply reform themselves."

"Abyssal fiends," Wulfsun muttered and tossed another sketch onto the small folding table in the center of the carriage.

"You do know of them, then?" Farah asked and her tone indicated surprise and even a trace of hope. "What is an abyssal?"

"They are creatures formed using magic from the Abyss. It's a realm that most aren't familiar with and has no real inhabitants like the other realms or even much fauna. In fact, from what we have been able to tell in the order, it might be nothing more than energy. This abyssal magic is similar to shadow magic in that it can copy things and has a dark bent, but it does more than simply copy. It is almost viscous when used and it seems to absorb—or more accurately consume—whatever it touches. I've been on a couple of missions into the realm. The topography, flora, and rocks all seem to be from different realms and are combined somewhat haphazardly there with dark traces left from the realm itself."

"The Abyss?" Devol inquired. "Isn't that where—ow!" He rubbed his side where Jazai had elbowed him. The diviner focused on him and tried to tell him to keep quiet but also nodded his head to give him a clue that he was right. That was where the Templar imprisoned the malefics.

"Then if you are familiar with it, can you deal with it?" Farah asked.

Wulfsun nodded. "More than likely, this isn't controlled by a single magi. I've yet to meet one who can wield it properly as one would any other type of magic. The reason these dark spots have been appearing all over is probably due to a tear."

"A tear?" Asla asked. "As in a tear between realms?"

"Aye. Someone tore a fissure open between our realm and that one." The Templar sighed and clenched his fist. "The dumb bastards. It would explain why they are stuck in one place and simply grow outward. The magic is slowly dripping into our realm as time goes on. It would also explain how you can hold it off with certain wards for a while but eventually, the abyssal magic will adapt or simply consume the wards and continue to expand."

"We've had that happen already," Farah admitted. "The

size of the spot was only around a hundred and fifty meters when we set the first wards up. It remained that way for about a week before the wards disappeared and it continued to grow. The scholars created more complex wards that halted the expansion again."

"And how long ago was that?" Wulfsun inquired.

"About ten days ago," she revealed and turned to look out the window. "We have another set of wards ready to go in case but they are the most complex wards they can muster. Even if they stop the dark spot from growing again, once those wards give out, there isn't anything else we can do." She pointed out the window. "You can see it from here."

The team peered in the direction she indicated. Over the next hill, a large dome sprawled across the land, pitch-black like light could not escape it. It stood tall and wide and was easily far bigger than the one hundred and fifty meters Farah had said it was at one point.

"How long did it expand for once the first set of wards collapsed?" Jazai asked.

"Only two days. Now, it measures at least four miles." She grasped her sword handle. "If this is a tear, we'll have to venture into it and find it to shut it, won't we?"

Wulfsun nodded solemnly. "Aye, and it is probably in the center of the blasted thing. This will certainly be a trip." He pointed to the three young magi. "If you have any food or drink, enjoy it now. Once we get inside, almost anything without magic will be suspect."

The three friends nodded, delved into their bags, and quickly devoured whatever food they carried. The carriage continued its trek. They were only a few minutes away and the abyssal dome loomed in front of them.

When they arrived, several guards surrounded the carriage quickly and only relaxed when Farah was the first to disembark. Wulfsun followed, then Asla, Jazai, and Devol, who hung onto the doorframe for a moment while he stared at the dome. This close, it seemed like it was swallowing the sky. His gaze settled on an archway that appeared to be made of cobalt with several intricate runes and wards etched into it. He finally stepped off and followed the others to where a group of scholars, guards, and soldiers waited.

"Captain Malik!" one of the guards exclaimed and saluted her. "I'm glad to see you ma'am. Is this the Templar?"

"It is, Haldt." Farah nodded. "And these are his soldiers. We're here to deal with the anomaly."

"His soldiers?" the guard asked and frowned as he studied the three young people. "They seem rather young. Is he sure about this?"

"I am," Wulfsun declared and all but bared his teeth at the guard. "They can handle this and have chosen to come here. Fortunately for you, I know how to deal with this accursed thing so if you would like us to get started on that, I suggest you move out of our way."

The guard, briefly taken aback, straightened quickly and nodded. "Y-yes, sir. This way."

"He knows how to deal with it?" one of the scholars

asked another. "Thank the Astrals. I had begun to fear what the possibilities would be if we couldn't contain it."

"Nothing good," the other scholar mumbled as the team passed them. "We'll have to ask him the specifics when they return."

"If," the first scholar replied.

Wulfsun shook his head. "Honestly, I would be more concerned if they did know what this was," he said, his tone low enough that he didn't broadcast it but the rest of the group could hear. "I'd hate to see what would happen if enough fame-hungry scholars decided to play with the Abyss to make a name for themselves."

"It could be what happened here," Farah pointed out as another scholar approached her with a box. "Scholars can be rather inept when they get impatient."

"Yes, and what folly they bring," Jazai muttered. "It's not like they are the ones typically responsible for discovering the full capabilities of magic or anything."

"Here you go, Ms. Malik." the new arrival said and opened the box to reveal several marbles. "These will take you back to the entrance once you break them. It will require a little vis to do so. We had to use a special container for the magic so we could apply small wards to defend them from some of the…irregularities that happen within."

"Thank you," Farah stated, took the box, and turned to the others. "Take one, each of you. As she said, these will teleport you back here in case something goes wrong."

"Or when we're done with this mess," Wulfsun added, took one of the marbles, and stowed it in a pouch. He looked at the scholar. "Do you have any idea where the center is?"

"Well, the dome stretches for a little more than four miles, so a couple of miles heading north." She pointed through the gate. "If the center of the dark spot is where it started to grow, that would be in the bloodflower patch."

"Bloodflowers?" Devol asked and looked at Asla.

"Yes, bloodflowers." The scholar nodded. "We have one of the largest fields of bloodflowers here in Renaissance and we use them in certain ceremonies, such as—"

"There's no need for a history lesson right now," Farah snapped and pointed to the archway. "Open the gate. We're going to head in."

"At once, Captain!" One of the guards nodded, motioned quickly to several magi, and pointed at the gate.

"Are you sure we don't need anyone else?" Farah asked and drew her blade. "I'm certain a few would volunteer and many of the soldiers here are also skilled magi."

"Things can get tricky in the Abyss," Wulfsun stated and punched one of his gauntleted fists into the other. "Illusions, those abyssal fiends, not to mention the way it twists and turns the terrain it consumes. It might seem like a good idea to go in with an army but keeping the group small is for the best. There is less of a chance of chaos resulting."

"Very well." She took a deep breath and nodded, and four magi began to deactivate the wards around the gate. "Prepare yourselves. We will enter now."

Devol drew his majestic, Achroma, and activated his anima. Jazai and Asla did the same, along with the Templar captain and Farah. As soon as the gate opened, the group entered cautiously one behind the other.

As they passed the threshold, they were bombarded by the abyssal energy. It began to swarm around them but Wulfsun activated his barrier and pressed forward. "Keep your anima up and higher than normal," he instructed. "Your mana will adapt. Once we get into the guts of this we'll be in the clear."

Achroma began to shine and Devol glanced at it and pressed on. He could barely make out a clearing ahead. Without hesitation, he moved to the front of the team and used the light to guide them. The abyssal magic pressed down on him but a flash of light from his blade seemed to carve through it until he stopped in an area surrounded by dark trees with blue leaves. "Is this normal, Wulfsun?" he asked as he studied the twisted forest. He received no response.

When he turned, no one stood behind him. His heartbeat raced for a moment before he focused and calmed himself. Wulfsun had said there would be tricks and the members of their team had probably been separated by the barrage from the magics. He shouldn't have pressed ahead. With a shrug of resignation, he turned again and his gaze settled on some kind of structure in the distance. It seemed like a logical destination and perhaps the others saw it as well and would meet him there. For now, though, he was alone with Achroma in this dark, foreboding realm.

CHAPTER TWENTY-TWO

Asla heard a hoot above that sounded like the cry of an owl and it caught her off guard. This was probably the first sign of life she had heard in this unnatural world since they stepped inside the dome. She looked up with a frown and squinted as she tried to find the source of the sound. Trees surrounded her completely and although leafless, the tops seemed to bend inward toward one another.

She scanned the sky beyond the twisted branches but found no signs of any owl or birds in general. Her frown deepened until she recalled that Wulfsun had said the abyssal magic would play tricks on them. She merely had not expected them to be so banal. Tentatively, she took a couple of steps forward and hoped she had not fallen too far behind, only to be greeted by a black, muddy terrain and several pieces of bone with none of her team around her.

"Hey, Jazai. Be sure to keep us informed about any of the big, bad illusions, yeah?" Wulfsun called. "You are the scholar of the group, after all." When he heard no reply, he shrugged and looked back. "It might have been a bad joke but you don't have to…" his words faltered when he realized he was alone.

"How the hell did we get separated?" The Templar growled his frustration and looked around for any signs of life. This could only be an illusion, he decided. During his previous ventures into the Abyss, he had never seen someone warped around the realm or anything similar. That said, given the present situation, he honestly had no idea what this was capable of in their world.

He took a deep breath and calmed himself. "They will be fine," he muttered and examined his surroundings. He stood in a ravine of some kind and a wind whipped around him as he looked at the jagged rocks that blocked the sight of the top of the dome. "They are skilled and have probably realized the same thing I have. I am sure they can manage well until I get to them."

The Templar released a small burst of mana to circle him and watched it carefully to see if it passed through anything or anyone. It simply swirled around him and didn't connect to anything. If there were any human bodies present, they somehow escaped detection.

"Is this only an illusion?" he asked, walked closer to one of the rock walls, and placed his hand against it. While it certainly seemed real, it was also unnaturally cold to the touch. It might indeed be an illusion but it somehow used the terrain to enhance the division between them.

"I don't think it is trying to kill us yet," he reasoned,

although he was not exactly sure if the magic was sentient. It might merely be replicating what the realm did. "This could also be it trying to pick us apart, though."

Wulfsun charged his gauntlets, pounded them together, and launched a blast of mana to shatter the rocks around him. He waited for the dust to settle and scowled when he saw no distortion or opening in the area. This would, he realized, be a pain.

"Well, this is unfortunate." Jazai scanned the area in search of his team while he tapped the side of his head in thought. "Illusion seems the most likely explanation. I doubt everyone was teleported without me noticing. Cloaking and silencing everyone else would also be possible, although I would have a better guess if I knew more about what the hells this is."

His attempt to identify the problem was interrupted by a bright light several yards away. He spun, held his hand up, and readied the cantrip-infused rings, but he was able to relax slightly when the light faded and Farah appeared.

"Well, there is one of you at least." He sighed and straightened, although a thought occurred to him. "Assuming you are you of course. My guess is that this is an illusion, so you could simply be another part of that."

The guard captain frowned and strode toward him. He held his ringed hand steady but waited for her—or potentially it—to do something. Rather than answer or offer any kind of display of proof, she did nothing more than raise her fist to rap him on his head.

"Gah! There are other ways of proving it, you know!" He yelped and rubbed his forehead. "You have physical form, at least."

"I'm real, young magi," she stated with a sigh. "As are you. This is an illusion and I had hoped to dispel it. It seems I was only able to break through mine."

Jazai's hands lowered slowly and his gaze darted around as a hypothesis began to form. "And are potentially caught in mine," he said, his voice low.

Farah regarded him curiously, "Hmm? What do you mean?"

The young diviner retrieved his tome and flipped through its pages. "I don't think we were caught in a single large illusion. If we had been, your plan might have worked. But my guess is that we are trapped in several smaller ones so instead, you only found me. This would mean that we could all be caught in separate illusions but there is a limit to what it can do, otherwise you would have simply been sent to another personal trap."

"I see," she responded cautiously and looked at her sword. "So should I keep trying to break through until we are all together again?"

Jazai finally found the page he was looking for and read it quickly before he frowned and turned more pages. "We'll consider it, but it is likely that even if it worked, we would be trapped again deeper into the forest. I believe this is meant to force us to waste our energy and magic. I'm not able to find the others even using my majestic, which means their animas are hidden from us."

"What's the purpose? To delay us?" Farah snorted in

irritation. "It's almost petty if that's the case. What makes you so sure?"

"I'm honestly not," he admitted. "I'm not sure how this place works and only have theories. But we aren't being attacked and the illusion isn't horrific by any means, so it probably isn't meant to…" A smile formed on his lips as he tapped something in the book. "Man, it has been so long since I bothered to use this. I guess Zier did have a good reason to teach it to me."

"Teach what?" she asked. "Do you have a plan?"

"I'm guessing the magic isn't 'alive' as such but is reacting to ours. In a way, it is a mirror and only forms in certain ways when there is another magic to react to." He placed his palms together and bowed his head. "Which hopefully means there aren't illusions on top of illusions. Before you waste considerable mana trying to hack through them all, let me test something."

"What are you doing?" the captain questioned as his body began to illuminate with blue light.

"I'll be right back," he stated and closed his eyes. "Watch over me for a moment, all right?"

"What for?"

"Projection!" he shouted before his body began to slump and Farah lunged to catch him.

With a swipe of her claws, Asla loosed another wave of her anima. Not much seemed to change from the last time, however. For a brief moment, the barrier around her fell but revealed only a slightly different alignment of trees, these with actual foliage. She hadn't caught sight of any of her comrades thus far and the fruitless attempts had begun to tire her. If she continued with these random blasts, she would drain her magic too quickly and wouldn't be able to keep this up.

"Asla?" Jazai called and she spun, surprised, and almost cut the forest down before her gaze settled on her friend—or, at least, a blue image of him.

"What the hells? Jazai?" She gasped and studied the projection warily.

"It's neat, right?" He waved his hands enthusiastically. "This cantrip allows me to make a projection of myself using mana. It helps with a few things but getting past illusions is what counts right now."

"Illusions? Plural?" she asked.

"Indeed. It's a pain, isn't it?"

"Honestly, I wish you had chosen a nicer avatar to meet me with." Asla sighed and lowered her claws to her side. "Seeing you in this form is somewhat unnerving."

"Sorry, but a pigeon or puppy is not available to me," he replied dryly. "It naturally takes the form I'm most familiar with and isn't an easy cantrip to use in the first place. I'm merely lucky I'm a diviner so doing things like this isn't so taxing for me. I suppose I can try to change the form or would you rather I used that time to help get you out of here?"

"Huh. Yeah…uh, thanks. Getting out sounds more appealing," she admitted and looked away for a brief moment. "So what do you need from me? I've attempted to break through but the illusion keeps reforming."

"You may simply be slicing through different illusions,"

Jazai told her. "But that's neither here nor there. Right now, we are separated but that doesn't mean we cannot interact. Farah should be able to use her magic to disrupt the illusion. She already found me," he explained. "I needed to get a look at you and find out how these illusions are working here." He extended a glowing hand. "Give me a small trickle of your mana. This will enable me to track you."

Asla nodded and stretched her hand forward to direct a trickle of her mana to him. It appeared as a small orange orb and sank into his hand. "All right. Stay here. I'll have Wulfsun do the same. With all your mana, I will be able to pinpoint where everyone is and Farah can bring us together again."

"Okay—but wait. Does that mean you already found Devol?" she asked.

Jazai shook his head. "I couldn't find him, I think he pushed ahead so we should probably hurry and regroup so we can go looking for him."

The wildkin nodded furiously. "I understand, yes—go!" At that, the diviner seemed to fade and she looked between the trees directly ahead of her. She wondered if the other trees with the blue leaves she had seen were perhaps in the area where Devol was.

The Templar launched another burst of mana but nothing gave beneath it. He sighed and decided his best choice would probably be to press forward and see if there was some kind of threshold or perimeter where the illusion ceased.

"Wulfsun!" a familiar voice shouted. He looked quickly to where a projection of Jazai floated toward him.

"Jazai?" he asked. "Are you using a projection? It's a clever choice. I assume it means this is definitely an illusion?"

"Mostly, it seems, but some of it is real." The diviner held his hand out. "Quick, give me a little of your mana. I already have some of Asla's. Me and Farah have a way to get through it."

The man nodded. "All right, here tak—wait a minute." He drew his hand back. "How do I know this isn't another part of the illusion?"

"Are you kidding me?" Jazai placed his hands against his body. "I'm literally composed of my own mana. Can't you sense it?"

"The Abyss is capable of all kinds of things," he pointed out and raised his eyebrow. "Do you have proof it is you?"

"I honestly don't have the time to rattle off a list," Jazai muttered and extended his hand a little farther. "But what does it matter? You like to gamble, so come on!"

Wulfsun snickered, sighed, and moved his hand toward him. "Well, I guess it's true. But hurry, will you?"

The diviner took his hand and drew some of his mana, and it formed a yellow orb within him. "I'm sure your plan would have been so much faster."

"Get going," the Templar snapped and the boy shook his head reluctantly and disappeared. The large man folded his arms and smiled for a brief moment. The apprentice was proving his worth, as much of a pain as he could be. He was certainly smart and gifted and deserved to be praised to his father the next time Wulfsun saw the man.

A few minutes passed and he wondered if something had gone wrong. He toyed with the idea of making another attempt, mainly to fill the time, but a bright flash of light erupted in front of him. With a muttered curse, he shielded his eyes but when it began to fade, he saw Asla, Jazai, and Farah emerge from the brightness.

"There you are. Well done!" He grinned broadly as he walked to them. "Now let's—wait. Where's Devol?"

"I couldn't find him," Jazai admitted. "He's probably deeper in, which means there is still one illusion left."

"Well then, get to him," the Templar ordered. "What? Did you need permission?"

The diviner shook his head. "No, but I wanted to bring us together before I set off. Besides, if he is farther in, we'll need to get Farah closer."

"Fair enough," he conceded. "How far in do you think he is?"

"I don't know but probably fairly deep." Jazai rolled his shoulders. "So while I search for him, I need you to do something."

Wulfsun nodded. "Aye, what do you need?"

Jazai held his arms up and his expression revealed that he was not amused by this request. "I need you to carry me."

CHAPTER TWENTY-THREE

Devol placed one hand in the pocket of his pants and stared at the building. It had the appearance of a sanctuary or temple. It was large—three stories tall—and the roof and spires above seemed to have eroded considerably, which suggested that it had been abandoned for years. Dark-blue lines pulsated along the walls and to the left of the entrance, statues of what appeared to be Samara and Finis, the Astrals of life and death, stood like silent sentinels.

"Hey, Devol!" The swordsman turned as what appeared to be a blue ghost approached him. He readied his blade but the spirit stopped suddenly and held its hands up. "Whoa—watch where you point that! A majestic can do damage to me in this form."

"Jazai?" He frowned and lowered his blade slightly. "What happened to you?"

"This is a cantrip. I'm using it to cross the illusions," the diviner explained and paused to look curiously at the structure. "What is that?"

"I don't know. It looks like a temple that might have

been here before this area was overtaken," the swordsman reasoned. "I'd hoped we could all meet here."

"It's not a bad plan, especially since I think you ended up on the correct plane." Jazai looked around and nodded. "This area isn't as twisted as the others, which means the rest of us might be the ones still in the illusion."

"Is there anything I can do to help?" he asked.

Jazai hesitated for a moment, his gaze fixed speculatively on his friend's sword. "Your majestic—try filling it with mana and releasing it behind me."

Devol, while he had no idea what he tried to accomplish, obliged and began to fill Achroma with his mana. The light within the blade brightened. The diviner moved his projection hastily behind him as the swordsman leaned back and swiped the weapon forward. The glowing blade sliced through the trees but more importantly, it cut through the fog of darkness that surrounded them.

"What in the hells?" Wulfsun cried as he and the others in the group suddenly appeared in the distance when the fog dissipated.

"Wulfsun!" Devol shouted and waved at him to get his attention. "How did you know that would work?" he asked the projection.

"I didn't," Jazai admitted. "But it seemed miraculous that you were the only one to not be trapped in an illusion. I merely assumed that your majestic played a part in that."

"Achroma, huh?" He looked at the sword with a mixture of pride and frustration. "I need to discover what it is capable of."

"No kidding." His friend floated away. "I'll be right back. Wait here."

The projection drifted to Wulfsun and floated onto his back. Jazai, now in his physical body, stretched his arms as the Templar dropped him casually. The two argued briefly, but Asla hurried to the young swordsman. "Devol, are you all right?"

"I'm fine, thank you," he said with a smile. "I didn't have a chance to get in any harm and haven't come across anything other than these weird trees and this temple."

"Samara and Finis?" Farah noted, her gaze fixed on the statues as she stopped behind Asla. "We don't have any temples outside the city. By the design, this looks like a temple you would see in Britana."

"There are two abyssal spots there," Devol stated and returned his attention to the building, "If this magic 'consumes' things like Wulfsun said, perhaps it is swapping elements from each of the spots somehow?"

"That would explain where the trees came from," the guard captain agreed and glanced over her shoulder. "And that rocky terrain we were in. I couldn't see the color of the stone, but it looked like some of the ravines you might find in Soel."

"It's good to see you in one piece, Devol!" Wulfsun said as he and the diviner caught up. "Jazai said it was you who dispelled the illusion."

"It was my majestic," he said and held the blade up. "It was Jazai's idea. I would never have thought to use it like that."

"It's probably best you start to," his friend pointed out with a glance at the blade. "Honestly, it's rather handy."

"Do you think we should have a look at the temple?" Farah asked Wulfsun.

The Templar captain nodded. "It's probably safer to do so and make sure nothing is hiding in there. But we have a fair distance to cover before we reach the center."

The team of magi approached the structure cautiously. Asla's ears twitched and Jazai's eyes glowed. Both remained alert and scanned their surroundings to be sure nothing snuck up on them. The fact that nothing did seemed to make them more on edge.

"It's too damn quiet," Wulfsun muttered and Devol had to agree. They had been in the dome for about ten or fifteen minutes now and besides the illusions and the blast of abyssal magic they had walked through, nothing had occurred. The area itself seemed almost sterile, merely dirt beneath them and the temple in front of them, with no wind or noise around.

A crack was immediately followed by a snap and something darted around the Finis stature. Asla bared her teeth and Devol held his blade up, but Jazai simply pointed his index finger at the shadowy being that attempted to hide and fired a mana missile at it. It struck home and the creature fell, but it seemed to wiggle for a moment before it lay still. The three of them ran closer to examine it.

The swordsman looked at the small, thin black body with three clawed fingers on each hand and tiny, curved legs that ended in three clawed toes. Its head was gaunt and small nubs dotted the top. One of its eyes was partially closed but revealed faded yellow eyes. "I think this is...a Jota?"

Jazai knelt and flicked one of its long ears. "It is, but I've never heard of one with this color."

"This place seems to darken everything within," Asla

commented and closed the imp's eye. "It is possible that this is an Osirian jota."

"The creatures stay together in packs." Farah planted her sword into the dirt and knelt beside the wildkin. She ran a hand over the corpse and noted deep gashes in the flesh. "This one was injured even before it was struck by the missile. It was hiding from something."

Wulfsun joined them and examined the wounds "These cuts aren't from any beast I am aware of. Not to mention that it seems steeped in this cursed magic."

"Was something trying to eat it?" Devol asked.

"I haven't the foggiest notion, honestly. This looks like something attacked it merely because it could. Anyone and anything knows that jotas can be trouble even on their own, but it is always near a pack. You should kill it in one strike or retreat." Wulfsun took a blade from his leather strap and peeled the edges of the wound back. "It's jagged and there are flecks of something in there."

"Of what?" Farah asked as Wulfsun removed his blade and took something from the tip.

He studied it with a frown where it remained stuck on his finger. "It appears to be...blood?"

"Well, given that it was cut open, it isn't a surprise, is it?" Jazai questioned.

"The jota's blood is still fresh. This is clotted and... black..." Wulfsun's words faltered and his eyes widened as he shook the congealed blood off his finger. "Ah, hells!"

A rumble issued from inside the temple. Those crouched beside the carcass straightened hastily and all except the Templar jumped back as he prepared a shield. A large, dark hand reached quickly from inside the temple, snatched the man, and began to drag him in.

"Wulfsun!" Devol cried before shocked shouts came from behind him.

"Agh!" He and Asla turned to where Farah and Jazai struggled with something on the ground. What looked like hands with shadowy claws had emerged from under the abyssal dirt to grasp their ankles and attempt to pull them down.

The diviner began to fire his cantrips at their attackers. One of the arms let go and he forced himself back. He heard a loud crack in the process and realized that he was almost free, but the arm still held fast to his ankle.

Farah pointed her blade at the soil and shouted in rage as she thrust her blade into the muck. A swirl of bright light coursed down it and into the earth. In the next moment, the ground ripped apart in a bright eruption and a being streaked out.

It looked like a person dressed in dark robes and pants, although the symbols on the robes were familiar. They were similar to those worn by the scholars at the entrance of the dome. Its arms were skeletal and curved at the fingers like talons. Farah tried to catch hold of it but was forced to let go when the being tried to cut her face. It shuffled along the ground, twisted, and reshaped itself before it stopped slowly, facing up. Both arms raised and curved into a frightening angle to stretch back, flatten its hands on the ground, and push itself up. It hobbled forward, its face obscured by the hood of the robe before it raised its head slowly to look at the rest of the group. The face was dark but had more definition than the sketches. It appeared starkly gaunt and had the same white eyes as the drawing.

"A fiend," Jazai said, his voice low enough to be almost a whisper as he extended his hand.

Two more dropped from above the temple. Asla felt a rumble beneath her and pushed Devol and Jazai out of the way when more hands thrust out to snatch them. They missed their quarry and the owners of the arms forced themselves from the dirt to glare balefully at the magi.

"Not merely a fiend," Devol muttered and the flames coursed over his body as Asla gathered herself. Farah let light surge along her blade and Jazai began to build his mana. "Many, many fiends."

"Look at their robes," the wildkin said and glanced at those behind them. "And the armor on those…"

"I guess we know what happened to everyone who was lost inside, huh?" Jazai grimaced and formed a shield as a couple inched closer. The beings crept around the group and their claws reached out as they stared blankly at them with hollow lights in their eyes. Their robes dragged along the ground, all in various states of disrepair, and pieces of the armor of others cracked under the strain of movement.

"Can they be saved?" Farah asked as they closed in.

"Unfortunately, I don't believe we'll have the chance for that," Devol stated and held his blade up. "We need to hurry and see what happened to Wulfsun."

The captain steadied herself, nodded, and sliced quickly through a fiend. Its body erupted in light and faded to nothing. Another swiped her arm and its claws scratched at her armor but bounced off. She placed her hand against its skull and fed her light magic into it. The being's eyes and mouth lit up as the magic surged within. It crumpled under her grasp before it turned into a dark fog that disappeared into the ground.

Asla fell on all fours and let her anima surge as it took the form of a feral cat. She launched herself at two of their adversaries and sliced each through their chest before they could even react to her approach. As she turned, they began to repair themselves so she doubled back and attacked in a flurry of fearsome scratches. The armor fell as they also turned into fog and dissipated into the sky.

A fiend leapt at Jazai but he knocked it away with the shield. When another attempted to strike him from behind, he blinked behind it and extended his ring finger. The ring flared and a mana blade formed around his hand and sank into his attacker's head.

"Shock!" He summoned an arc of electricity and sent it through the blade and into the fiend. It neither twisted nor flinched but began to stretch its hands toward him. He grunted, pulled the blade back as two more shambled closer to him, and raised a palm. "Pulse!" A wave of mana blasted out in front of him and hurled the three away. "Elemental magic doesn't work on them. Be careful."

"It's not a big concern for me," Devol replied and thrust his blade into an armored being, which filled and erupted with light similar to Farah's magic. "If you need help, let me know."

"Show off." Jazai snorted and pointed his pinky at the recovering fiends. Chains were summoned around the three of them and he held both hands up. "Blast." A large mana orb appeared in front of his palm and when he fired it at the creatures, they were instantly engulfed by it. The sphere erupted and the robes and armor scattered to leave only the dark fog that drifted into the trees.

Farah felt a sharp pain in her side and turned toward a half-destroyed fiend, a shadowy trail left under its chest, that had managed to inflict a small cut on her ribs. "Someone needs to finish their work!" she yelled and knocked it aside before she stabbed her blade into its head.

"It might have been me. My apologies!" Asla called and noticed two of the enemy that crept forward behind the light-magic-user. She slid her hand to the quiver Roko had given her, removed an arrow, and loaded it into the crossbow on her arm. Calmly, she fired the bolt and controlled it so it pierced the heads of both beings and stalled them. "Farah, behind you!"

The swordswoman spun and cleaved through the two. She nodded in thanks to the wildkin once she'd finished off her would-be ambushers.

Devol had become separated from the group and a line of fiends advanced on him. The distance from his teammates worked for him as he had no need to worry about where the others were when he attacked. He lifted his sword, built his mana up, and stretched the weapon skyward before he arced it at his enemies. The blade lengthened into a large blade of light that sliced the beings in half where they stood. They immediately turned into fog and disappeared into the ground or the air. He frowned as he watched it. Something was odd about the dark vapor but he would have to explore that later.

"I'm going find Wulfsun!" he shouted and sprinted to the temple. "Can you hold?"

"We'll be fine," Farah responded. "Whatever snatched him was far bigger than these annoyances. Find him!"

Devol nodded and ascended the stairs to the temple quickly. Once he stepped through the entrance, the doors slammed shut behind him and he was left in the dark. A loud shout from below sounded distinctly like Wulfsun. The boy found a large hole in the main chamber, and without hesitation, he leapt into it, hoping to find his mentor within.

CHAPTER TWENTY-FOUR

Devol charged his anima as he plunged into a cavern below the temple. He landed with a splash in a shallow pool of water and used vis to compensate for the impact.

Even with the aid of his mana, his legs gave way and pain surged through his ankles and calves. "Wulfsun. Are you alive?"

"Devol, get down!" the Templar shouted and the boy ducked reflexively as something large flew overhead. He turned quickly to look for whatever had attacked him as his mentor splashed through the water toward him.

"What was that?" He gasped, retrieved his sword hastily from where he'd dropped in the shallow pool, and held it up.

"I haven't been able to get a good look at it." Wulfsun checked the boy and the rest of his gear. "But it didn't look like any beast I know and it is bloody massive."

Devol stood and began to walk to the bank. "I saw its eyes. It didn't have any irises, only a blank void of white like the fiends above."

"So there are fiends, then?" The Templar dug in his satchel and removed three red orbs. "Let's hope they weren't too badly damaged. I fell down here while fighting this blasted creature." He lobbed them into the air and they hovered in place and illuminated with a bright red light. "I have a couple more but should probably save them in case this goes on for a while."

The swordsman scrambled onto a pile of rocks and took a moment to catch his breath. "It looked huge—at least ten to twelve feet tall. Something like that shouldn't be able to hide so easily."

"Despite its size, it is a fast beastie." Wulfsun looked at the hole high up in the ceiling. "I'm not sure we want to fight down here. Can you make it up there?"

"You're by far the heavier of the two of us," Devol replied as he studied the aperture carefully. "I can probably make it if I can get good footing. Do we want this beast to follow us to the surface, though?"

"Are you worried about the others?"

He nodded. "They are already dealing with the fiends. While they are not all that troublesome, there are many of them. If you have fought with this beast for this long, it must be dangerous."

"I merely have a hard time landing a strike on the dammed thing," the Templar muttered. He looked up as the surface on which they stood began to shake. "Here it comes."

The creature came from below, launched from under the water, and scattered most of it, it seemed to swallow a fair amount of it as well.

"Watch out!" Devol yelled. Once they were close to the

water's edge, they turned to face their attacker and both felt a similar shock when the beast was illuminated by the lighting orbs.

They stared at an abomination of scaled, sinewy muscle. It had two large arms with four claws that dug into the rocks. The large body was wide and chunky with cracked ridges along its chest and shoulder. It tapered into a long snake-like tail that drove its slithering motion. A bulbous head topped the body, and the white eyes the boy had noticed before peered coldly at them. Its mouth seemed like it was made less for function and more as a container for sharp, jagged teeth.

"By the Astrals, what is that?" He gasped.

Wulfsun saw a darkened glow beneath its scales and skin. The odd eyes and the dark spots that seemed to travel along its body brought a recollection to him. "This is an abyssal beast, lad. It's an amalgamation of other beasts forced into one decrepit shell."

"An abyssal beast?" Devol looked at the dark creature and tightened his hold on his majestic. "We can still destroy it, right?"

The man was silent but with a glance, Devol saw the determination in his mentor's face. "Aye, and we have to. We don't want this to follow us, do we?"

He shook his head. "All right, let's—" Devol did not have the time to complete his suggestion. The beast released the walls it was balancing on and plunged toward them with an open maw. Without a cry or a roar and with merely a showing of teeth and tongue, it dove into a vicious assault.

The boy turned to leap but saw Wulfsun take a firm stance to stab at the creature. "Wulfsun, watch yourself!" he cried but the Templar remained steadfast and raised his barrier when it drew frighteningly close. It pounded into the shield, bit down on it, and ripped at it with its claws.

Devol saw an opportunity. He turned and lunged at the monster while it was busy trying to reach Wulfsun, held his sword up, and thrust the blade into its side. It slid deep and flooded it with light. The beast released the barrier and flung itself to the side. The sword came free and he braced himself against the loss of weight on the blade.

The Templar nodded to him as he dropped his barrier. "It looks like you'll be extremely useful with this one," he told him, a little out of breath. They turned and froze when they noticed something swirling in the beast's mouth. "What in the—"

The creature spewed a torrent of abyssal magic directly toward them.

"Hells!" they both cried and used vis to race away. Their adversary vaulted onto the wall and landed with a dull thud. It burrowed inside and vanished. They came to a halt a few yards away and Devol breathed deeply while Wulfsun growled as he cracked his knuckles.

"Devol, are you all right?" he asked through rapid breaths. "Are you already winded after a little run?"

"I'm fine." The swordsman grunted as he stood. "I'm a little taken aback, is all. This place is something quite strange so far but it appears we've learned one thing." He looked at his sword. "My blade can damage it, at least consistently. It was the same with the fiends above. They explode with light like with Farah's magic."

"That abyssal fire or whatever it is will be a problem, though," the Templar muttered. "I don't even want to try to use my shields against that as I'm not sure what good it would do."

"Maybe I can behead it or cut it into pieces," Devol suggested. "If you can get it into position, I should have enough time to—" The ground began to rumble again and he looked down and saw the dark, ink-like magic seeping through the cracks.

Wulfsun grabbed his arm and flung him away before he jumped the other way. A jet of abyssal magic broke through the ground before the beast emerged, turned, and focused on the Templar with its teeth bared. "Whatever your plan is, go for it. I'll stall this creature."

"I'm on it," Devol muttered through gritted teeth, held Achroma up, and strengthened his anima. He ran to the rock mound and glanced over his shoulder as the monster dove from overhead and struck at the large man. The Templar jumped to the side and ran back a little as he raised his shields and let his adversary swipe at him before he countered with a punch to its side. The blow knocked it back but it simply spun in the air and swooped at him again.

The young swordsman continued to build his mana up but the beast and Wulfsun had moved farther away in their struggle. He wasn't sure if he could reach it now and decided he had to get closer. He leapt onto the water and glided across it with some vello control. When he heard a yell, he turned to where his mentor now careened across the cavern, having most likely been swatted by the creature's tail. He tightened his hold on the hilt of his sword, leapt forward, and slid down a pile of rocks to the ground. While he would have preferred a more stealthy approach, he had no other options and Wulfsun would die if he didn't get there.

He almost froze when the beast reared and its mouth filled with magic again. Devol's eyes widened and he wondered desperately if he was close enough. Even the Templar was not sure if his barriers were enough to stop that magic. He held the sword with both hands, filled it with as much mana as he could muster, and hoped to force it in rather than guide it.

The monster turned toward him and revealed its many lines of teeth again as it slithered closer and opened its mouth to fire the abyssal stream. It extended its head toward him and he vaguely heard Wulfsun cry his name. He raised the blade and released the stored mana as the beast unleashed its magic. Light consumed his vision and he held his breath and closed his eyes.

The blade lowered to a full stop and Devol's eyes remained closed. He felt nothing but in the darkness, he heard a loud splash as something landed in the water. The beast began to wail in pain. When he opened his eyes and looked down, his mouth dropped open. The blade glowed with a brilliant light that ran through the entire sword, the abyssal magic was gone, and the illumination from the majestic lit up the cavern. The blade, hilt, and guard all sparkled like new and glimmered brightly. Not only that, but he felt rejuvenated like his mana had gone from a still pool to a flowing fountain.

"Devol!" Wulfsun shouted. "I don't know what you did but by the Astrals, keep doing it."

"I don't know what I did either," he shouted in response.

"Look out!" the Templar warned and ran forward as he gathered his mana into his gauntlets.

The boy whirled toward the creature that once again surged forward with its mouth open to devour him. With a yell, he raised the sword and swung it and a flash of light blocked his vision.

The cavern became suddenly and uncomfortably silent. Devol drew a deep breath, startled when he saw the inside of the beast's maw in front of him, and took a few hasty steps back. The beast didn't move and he frowned and focused on a white line on the top of its mouth. The line separated slowly and the creature fell into two halves that shook the ground with their impact. Despite his new influx of life from the sword, he fell to his knees. Unbelievably, he had slain the monster.

Splashes behind him drew him back to reality as Wulfsun ran up to him. "You did it, Devol. Well done, boy!"

"That's it?" he asked and breathed deep. "The beast is dead? Are you sure? The fiends outside would turn to—" They stood side by side and stared as it began to melt into the inky liquid the boy had come to know as abyssal magic. The entire creature disintegrated and formed viscous strands of the magic that combined into a small blob. It floated through the hole in the ceiling.

"That can't be good." Wulfsun helped Devol to his feet. "Come on. Let's see how the others are doing."

The boy nodded. Although he felt his mana had been rejuvenated, he still struggled with extreme weariness. He frowned at the hole and tried to decide if he could even attempt the leap.

"Do you need some help?" the Templar asked and caught hold of the back of his coat.

"Wulfsun—wait. What are you doing?" The man made no response but picked him up and drew his arm back as he pointed at the hole with his other hand.

Devol's eyes widened when he realized what was about to happen. "Control yourself. There's no need to use too much—" Wulfsun tossed him through the hole and into the temple. His instincts fortunately kicked in and he flipped himself and directed mana into his legs seconds before he pounded into the ceiling. Imprints of his boots were left when he pushed off the tiles and landed on the floor in the main chamber, his legs shaking.

He looked at the hole as he dragged in a breath. The Templar had managed to jump high enough to catch hold of the edges of the hole. He pulled himself through quickly and dusted himself off. "I should have brought a towel," he muttered and looked at Devol with a wide grin. "Fancy footwork there! I might have used a little too much vis, I think. The distance looked farther than it was."

Devol's legs continued to shake slightly but he nodded and thanked him for the assistance. "We should go check on the others, right?"

"Right! Let's get movin'," Wulfsun declared and slapped the young magi's back enthusiastically. "I want to make sure that beastie is dead."

CHAPTER TWENTY-FIVE

When Devol and Wulfsun stepped cautiously out of the temple, they saw the others looking up at something that held their attention. They did the same, startled, as the ooze-like remains of the beast congealed into a large orb before it erupted and scattered large amounts of the dark fog around the area. They all held their mouths or sucked in their breath with the exception of Wulfsun, who began to yell, "Calm yourselves! It's all right." He held his arms outstretched and his palms up. "It won't hurt ye but keep your anima up."

The young swordsman lowered his hands as the abyssal fog drifted around him and finally sank into the ground. "What is it doing? All the fiends turned into this too after we killed them."

"It's the abyssal magic," Wulfsun explained as the others regained their composure. "It's something…unique it does. It seems to recycle itself in some manner."

"Don't all forms of magic do that?" Jazai asked and

peered at the dome as some of the remnants began to stick to the roof.

"Magic replenishes and mana reforms, but only if there is enough to start with," the Templar replied. He folded his arms as he focused on a trail of the remains that drifted in front of his eyes. "You create a mana missile and fire it, and once it hits, it disappears. This stuff…I am not sure what happens exactly but it leaves trace amounts that are simply absorbed into other concentrated pieces of it. It happens in the abyssal realm too and much more quickly than here. It's one of the reasons why you don't wanna stay there too long. No matter how many of those bastards you slay, more keep coming and simply reappear right behind ya."

"So it possesses bodies in its own world as well?" Farah asked. "Who lives there?"

"Possess?" Wulfsun asked, looked around, and finally noticed the bodies around them. "Aw, hells. Were these some of yours?"

"They were." She nodded. "Our soldiers and scholars who were deployed here. It seems like the magic possessed their corpses, similar to how ghouls function."

"I can't get away from those bastards," Wulfsun grumbled as he knelt and examined one of the bodies. "Aye, but in the abyssal realm, that only happens if someone falls. They can simply create constructs in different forms to attack, but they all seem humanoid to some extent— although I would say it is closer to demonic."

"More like the pictures we saw on the way here?" Asla asked.

Wulfsun dropped the body and nodded, "Aye. This probably wasn't meant to be a real attack. I think this substance simply makes things at random. Although, given that beast and the possession of these soldiers and guards, this could possibly have been a way to defend itself."

"Defend itself?" Devol asked and turned to his mentor. "Wulfsun, you say that like this is alive and giving orders."

The Templar shrugged and checked the fit of his gauntlets. "It may not be alive in the traditional sense, boyo, but there's something to this magic—something that makes me glad it's not my profession that has to experiment with it." He turned and nodded to Jazai. "My condolences."

"I beg your pardon?" the diviner countered before Farah stepped in.

"We need to get the rupture that has enabled this closed," she stated and put her blade away. "And as quickly as possible. If this…anomaly is reacting to us, it will only continue to escalate so we should deal with it before it gains strength."

Wulfsun nodded. "Agreed. Fortunately, I think this will be far easier than a trip into the realm itself. It only has a finite amount of the substance to work with but still, it's best to not press our luck." His mana flared as he cracked his knuckles "Stay close to me. We're gonna rush through the rest of this. Jazai and Farah, make sure we don't get caught in another of those damned illusions aye?"

The two nodded. The boy checked his rings while Farah held a hand out and formed an orb of light, which she cast out in front of them. "That will shine through any illusion, assuming we're not trapped in one at the moment. Make sure you always stay within sight of it."

The others exchanged glances to make sure they were

all ready. Wulfsun leaped on top of the Temple and gestured for them to hurry. "Let's get the job done, ladies and gents!"

"Hey, Markus," a guard by the name of Henry began and pointed behind his comrade. "Are we expecting any more support or new arrivals today?"

"Not to my knowledge," Markus responded and turned to see what he was pointing at. "Why do you— Who the hells is that?"

Five figures approached from over the hill, all dressed in dark garb, but the one who walked in front had no hood and wore red shades. Their stride was swift and they marched directly to the dome with no hesitation.

"Civilians?" Henry asked.

His teammate shrugged. "Who knows, but they aren't supposed to be here. Hey, Tobias—incoming!" Another guard, along with several others and a few scholars, looked at the approaching group. Tobias told a couple of guards to follow him. He had planned to simply stop them and tell them to turn back, but something was odd about them. Did he need to warn them about the massive darkness stretching before them?

Unfortunately, Tobias and the guards would not have their chance to question the strangers. He raised a hand to signal for them to halt and the leader of the group did the same. The man pointed some kind of stick with a red crystal in the tip in their direction. A flash emitted from this and the guards were incinerated before they even had a moment to scream.

The other guards snatched their arms up and some scholars ran while others prepared spells. The four beings behind the fire mage suddenly sprinted forward and caught some knights in the front. They used daggers or the unnatural claws on their fingers to pierce through or around the armor to eliminate them with quick strikes.

Salvo grinned as he formed several small orbs of fire that he cast at random targets. Some were able to defend against them with shields, both enchanted and mana-created, and others were able to dodge them. Two fell to the fiery onslaught. He twisted his wand and commanded the flames that now burned the grounds to snake around and envelope more guards as his ghouls continued their attacks.

The swift onslaught and growing fire caused massive disarray amongst the defenders. Salvo noticed a pair of scholars trying to escape on his left side. He flicked his wand toward them, ensnared them in a cage of fire, and held a finger up to tell them to wait as he continued to deal with the rest.

"Someone needs to contact the others inside!" Haldt cried "They need to know—watch out!" He held a shield up and a torrent of fire slammed into it. The flames began to spin and grow to consume him and two other guards beside him. Their armor was quite convenient for Salvo. It meant they could not run away as effectively, which might have been rather annoying.

The fire mage finally approached the dome and stared at

it in amusement. "This is only a trial run?" he remarked as he spun his wand carelessly. "I wonder what he has planned for the real thing. This seems nothing more than a novelty." He looked at the ghouls and pointed to one. "You—go to that cage and fetch me a scholar. Slit the other." The ghoul nodded and hurried to the fiery cage as Salvo let it fall. When he felt a thumping in the box on his waist, he opened the container, took the mask out, and smiled pleasantly at it.

The ghoul brought one of the scholars, who was a sputtering mess from the ordeal. Salvo nodded to the gate. "Open it."

"You can't be serious!" the prisoner babbled. "You want to go in there? You have killed anyone here who has any chance to contain it."

"It works as well," he muttered and traced the etchings on the mask. "It wasn't my goal but it benefits my master all the same."

"You know who did this?" the scholar asked, equally aghast and angry. "What are you trying to do to our kingdom?"

"If it makes you feel any better, he's after the world as a whole, I think. He's been rather vague about that," Salvo admitted and turned to look at the kneeling man. "Now, open the gate or I will after I dispose of you slowly and painfully."

Although he was shaking, the man grasped his knees and shook his head. "You intended to do that anyway. Like hell I'll willingly do anything for you."

He gave the man a wide grin and turned the mask as he took his shades off and slid them into a pocket. "Well, you are certainly right about that first part." He placed the mask on his face. The scholar raised an eyebrow briefly before his eyes widened in fear as the mask seemed to reshape itself and assume a darker visage of its wearer. The fire mage pointed his wand at the head of the scholar, who closed his eyes and said a prayer to the Astrals before the red crystal of Salvo's majestic flared and the man's body was turned instantly to ashes.

"Huh." The large man looked at his wand and tapped the side of his mask. "I didn't mean to do it so fast. This is a powerful little accessory, isn't it?" He looked at the emotionless ghoul and sighed. "Why am I asking you? Let us go and find our real prey." He turned to the gate and burned the runes off before he blasted the shield until it shattered. The darkness held within spilled past him and enveloped the area.

Salvo began to shiver in anticipation. Even amongst all this strange magic, he could feel them not too far off. He heard himself laugh which was uncharacteristic of him, but he didn't bother to stop. Single-minded and determined, he marched into the dome and the ghouls followed. A voice in his head repeated only two words—*kill them*.

CHAPTER TWENTY-SIX

The group raced through the abyss, now in an area that brought to mind a crop field in the midst of decay. Above them, the clouds began to disperse but didn't fade away for some reason and instead, thickened and expanded to blanket the whole sky.

Devol could feel the magic that powered everything. Different types of magic felt different, but none were truly anything other than slight variations—a pressure, a small heat, a haze similar to walking into fog or smoke, all things that typically, only those with considerable experience would notice as peculiar or a sign.

But this was different. A feeling of heaviness permeated the entire area, not only his body. As he ran, he felt he not only had to run with extra weight attached to him but also as if he had to push through something that tried to keep him away.

Both Asla and Jazai's breathing began to labor like his did. Was this merely an effect of the abyssal magic now that they were closer to the center? Or was it caused by the presence of something else within? This was more tangible than anything he had fought or witnessed before.

As they drew closer to the center of the field, Devol pushed himself to go faster and so was the first to break through. A massive pit yawned in front of him, at least a quarter of a mile wide but incredibly deep. Obelisks floated around a large, swirling abyss in the center of the clearing and purple and red runes glowed before their color began to dim.

"What is this?"

Wulfsun's jaw clenched as he shook his head. "It is what I suspected, lad—a rift or a tear between dimensions. Those obelisks must be a part of some type of ritual they used to cause it."

"So if we destroy the obelisks the tear will close?" Farah asked and unsheathed her blade. She rolled the sleeves of her jacket up and lunged at one of the obelisks as the others finally joined them. The bright glow of her light magic swirled around her hands and into her blade as she tried to pierce one of the stones.

"Farah, don't!" the Templar shouted but she already had. The runes flared, turned white, and something struck her chest. She was catapulted back and thankfully, was caught by Jazai and Devol before she could make impact with the earth.

Her blade flared as she stood. She held it aloft and readied herself for another attempt to destroy one of the obelisks, but Wulfsun ran in front and blocked her path.

"Stop it, woman!" he shouted. Even at full volume, his words were barely audible above the roar of the wind and the unnatural howl that issued from the portal.

"Destroying the obelisks won't do anything right now. If we had destroyed them before the rift was opened, that might have been useful but at this point, they are what is holding it together."

"Then what would happen if we destroyed them? Wouldn't that close the tear?" Asla asked.

"Not necessarily. It's hard to tell but the tear may be sustaining itself. If anything, destroying the obelisks will cause the rift to grow wild. It might slow it temporarily but could also cause it to tear even more," he explained.

Farah pursed her lips but nodded and lowered her blade. Devol steadied himself and they peered at the scene below. The rift Wulfsun spoke of appeared to be similar to a portal, but the edges were jagged and the form twisted. Something was visible inside. "Wulfsun, what is that?!" he asked and pointed below. "Something is in there. Is that normal?"

"Ah, hells!" The Templar growled and thumped his gauntlets together. "There should be more of the magic pouring through. I had hoped it was dying down but something is blocking it. Something is coming through."

"And what is that?" Farah demanded.

They did not have to wait long to find out. A large hand was the first thing to emerge from the rift. It pushed against it as if it was some kind of muck and the earth simply wrapped around it. A second arm followed, then pointed horns on a head with no clean features. The being was the ebon shade of the portal.

Finally, the creature uttered a snarl and bellowed as it forced the rest of itself through. Jazai fell and placed his hands on the ground, and an earthen wall arose around them. Wulfsun added his barrier to it. A burst of magic was unleashed that shattered the wall and hurled them into the fields.

Devol landed and tumbled for a few moments before he turned and froze when a stream of purple lightning seared toward him. Asla leapt forward, snatched the back of his jacket, and flung them both away from the deadly assault. Remnants of the energy crackled on the soil and shifted between shades of purple and blue. He stared at it, both mesmerized and unnerved, before he moved his hand cautiously closer to it. Even without touching it, he knew there was something wrong about it. It burned, but when he jerked his hand back and ran the other one over it, his palm felt chilled.

The swordsman stood, shook the pain off, and helped Asla up. "Thanks for that," he said gratefully as they ran to the clearing. Wulfsun and Farah were already there and Jazai blinked in behind them. As they gazed at the being, the darkness faded and was replaced by a dark-blue skin. White eyes formed with slits for irises.

What had first appeared to be a pair of horns were two —one pair that pointed to the sky and one each on either side that curved around its head. A vertical mouth had rectangular husks around its lips that peeled back to reveal long, spear-like teeth. It stood on four legs and two long, spindly arms were coated in the abyssal energy it had fired at them and that traced through its chest and up to its shoulders.

The odd eyes finally cleared and it lowered its head and focused on the group. Devol could see nothing that might indicate fury, confusion, glee, or anything of that nature.

This being seemed to be as mindless as the beast he and Wulfsun had slain but he was not sure if he could even read the emotions of this one. It arched its back and stretched its legs and standing at full height, it was at least ten feet tall. As they stared at it in stupefaction, it leaned away from the group and several small holes beneath its eyes flared. Was it smelling them? Could these abyssal creatures even do that?

Finally, it uttered a gurgled hiss, snapped its mouth closed, and extended both arms. Wulfsun and Farah were the first to react. The Templar battered the large hand away with a solid punch while Farah sliced through the other arm. Her light magic drew another hiss from the creature. It stepped back and its large legs shook the ground when it stumbled.

"I don't know if you guys are standing around thinking of a clever plan!" Wulfsun shouted at Devol and his friends. "But now isn't the time for that. Kill this bastard!" He condensed his mana into one of his gauntlets and released a blast. The demonic creature swiped a hand and a surge of abyssal magic swallowed the attack. The man cursed as he prepared to charge before the demon leaned forward, planted its hands on the ground, and shrieked at the group.

Asla curled into a ball to block the sound and it almost deafened Devol. He looked at Jazai, who tried to fire a spell from one of his rings, but whatever it was simply vanished before it could form properly. The Templar stood tall, pounded his hands together, and released a large blast of mana that seemed to counter the demon's wail. He then responded with a roar of his own as he lunged forward and struck it in the chest with sufficient force to thrust it back by several feet.

The young diviner was finally able to fire a volley of mana bolts that pierced the creature as it tried to reengage. Asla shook her head and staggered to her feet but seemed to have recovered. Devol drew Achroma and joined Farah and they both raced toward the demon and struck. This turned out to be quite effective, as each of their attacks claimed one of its arms. The limb he'd severed began to disintegrate, only for the remnants of the magic to streak past him and back onto the demon. Farah's did the same and they shook their heads in disbelief as the creature's arms grew back. It turned toward them and lightning formed in its hands.

As Wulfsun ran forward for another blow, the being lifted its two back legs and kicked at him. The Templar caught the legs but was dragged to the ground. The demon fired a large chain of lightning at Devol and Farah. She drove her blade into the earth and erected a shield in front of them. The lightning bounced off and struck the soil around them, which erupted in geysers of the abyssal magic.

Asla had finally recovered enough to join the brawl. She bounded high and dove toward the demon's head with her claws extended. It evaded her but she was able to use her majestic to tear a chunk out of its neck and shoulder, which quickly reformed as it attempted to snatch her. The reaching arm was trapped in a mana chain held by Jazai. "Pulse!" he cried and sent a pulse of magic through the chain that blew the demon's arm off, albeit with the same results as before.

"Well, damn," the magi protested as he blinked next to Devol. "I should have gone for the head."

"I'm hoping that will work," his friend replied and Achroma flared in his hands.

"This beast is persistent!" Farah shouted and yanked her blade out of the ground.

Something caught Devol's eye and he turned quickly. Several smaller creatures pushed through the rift below.

"Wulfsun, more are coming," he shouted as the Templar finally recovered and forced the demon's leg out from under it. "You have to close the portal!"

"I doubt this damned thing will leave us be!" the man responded as he prepared to face the regenerating creature again. "I need to be able to focus when I work on the rift."

Devol turned to Jazai and Asla, who immediately understood and nodded as their animas strengthened. "We'll take care of it. You and Farah close that tear before we are overwhelmed."

"Are you sure, lad?" The Templar held his barrier against a blast from the beast before he grasped its arm and hurled it several feet away. "Can you handle it?"

"Of course," the swordsman assured him and he and Asla charged into the fray before the creature could recover.

"It's probably better than what you two have to deal with." Jazai joked morbidly as he fired a missile at the head of the demon. Wulfsun and Farah looked into the pit, where at least a dozen fiends pushed through with more behind them.

"Can we still seal it at this point?" she asked and looked somewhat dubiously from her sword to the enemy below.

"Aye, we can. It will take some doing, though." He adjusted his left gauntlet and nodded to her. "You got my back?"

Farah rested her blade on her shoulder and nodded. "I am ready, Captain."

"Ha!" The Templar chortled and bent at the knees as he prepared to leap. "That's good to hear, Captain." The two of them jumped into the pit to face the horde that now had their complete attention.

CHAPTER TWENTY-SEVEN

Wulfsun swung a powerful single punch smash into the face of one of the oncoming fiends, which released a ripple of magic that surged through a group behind it. Farah quickly began her attack. She sliced through two in one swing before she spun and drove her blade into the head of the next, then used her light magic to extend the tip of her blade and skewer another behind it.

"They are hardly a challenge." She growled and kicked the being off her blade as she readied herself for another wave of them.

"These are small fry," the Templar replied and stamped a boot onto a fallen fiend. "They are probably pouring in because of all the ruckus the big guy made getting here."

She held her sword back, charged it with light magic, and sliced deftly at her new targets. Her blade was now a glowing saber that cleaved through five of the creatures before they had time to even get within range to attack.

Wulfsun chuckled as he caught the hand of an attacker

and thunked it into the earth before he hurled it at another to thrust both back into the rift. "You're exactly like the lad," he told her and climbed quickly over some unsteady terrain as he approached the tear. "If you were a Templar, you would make a good mentor for him as well."

"That blade of his...he doesn't use holy magic, does he?" she inquired as she kicked the feet out from under another fiend before she smoothly beheaded one that tried to attack her from behind.

"Not exactly," Wulfsun admitted, checked his satchels, and shook his head. "Damn. Ah well, Plan B then."

The guard captain noticed two of the fiends sliding down the sides of the pits from above. She pointed her blade at them, funneled her magic through it, and unleashed a bolt of light magic that erupted beside them. Both were soon covered in the glowing, ethereal magic before their forms collapsed into the dark fog. "Is something the matter?"

"I forgot a reagent," he admitted as he sidled closer to the rift. His anima strengthened to protect him against the disruptive abyssal magic. "There's no need to worry, though. I have a better plan." He held his gauntlets up. Both glowed brightly, almost blindingly so. "You've got my back, right, Captain?!"

Farah leapt beside him and struck a fiend down on landing. "Of course."

The Templar nodded, positioned his gauntlets over the rift, and extended them to either side. Two mana constructs that took the form of his gauntlets appeared on the edges of the rift. He began to pull inward and although he wasn't holding anything in his arms, he struggled as he drew his hands together. Farah watched as the rift was forced closed by the magical gauntlets.

"What do you intend to do? Hold it closed forever?"

"I only need to shut it," Wulfsun shouted in response. "After that, I can set a ward up to keep it shut and you can destroy the obelisks."

"So I wasn't completely wrong then," she muttered and scowled at several fiends being reborn from the abyss. She held her sword up and checked her surroundings to make sure no others were sneaking around them or coming in from above. They were numerous but easy prey and she wondered how the young ones above were faring.

"This bastard is the worst!" Jazai shouted before he blinked away as the abyssal demon attempted to crush him underfoot.

"It heals itself too quickly," Asla added but continued to rip and tear pieces of the creature apart with little success. The wounds she inflicted were healed almost as soon as she made them. "We can knock it down but I do not believe it feels real pain."

"It keeps making those gurgles and hisses," Devol pointed out. "It has to feel something."

"I think it only does that because it can't swear at us," the young diviner responded. He checked his tome but grunted in annoyance when he found nothing useful. "It doesn't even register."

"I think we'll simply have to hit it with enough force for it to not have a chance to regenerate," the swordsman said.

Jazai nodded and wiped his brow. "I hate it when brute force is the correct choice." He took a deep breath and regulated his anima. "I have a plan."

"You do?" he asked. Asla yelled at them to move and they realized that the demon had begun to charge another blast of magic. Devol prepared to defend but noticed something odd. A bright spot appeared on its torso and grew larger, and its chest began to protrude. He felt oddly hot and wondered if this was some new magic the beast possessed.

It turned but its chest erupted in flames before it could finish. They spread quickly to cover its whole frame. It attempted to repair itself but the fire simply continued to grow larger and hotter and soon, the creature couldn't keep up. The three friends watched as the abyssal demon fell and even the fog could not escape the flames.

Devol looked at his comrade, who noticed this and shrugged. "That wasn't me. I have no idea what—"

"Someone is approaching," Asla warned as she stepped beside them. Four figures in dark robes like those he'd seen at the station moved steadily toward them. They were ghouls, he realized, surprised to see them there. He grasped his majestic and stepped forward, but Jazai caught his shoulder and held him back.

"Devol...it's him—the fire magi from Rouxwoods," he stated with a grimace. "I recognize the mana but something is different. It's erratic and...darker."

"Darker?" Devol turned as a fifth figure emerged from the field. He recognized the wand immediately—the one Vaust called Kapre—and he recognized something else too that made his eyes widen.

"That's the mask," Asla whispered and crouched beside them. "The mask the monster wore."

"The demon mask." Jazai nodded. "It's a malefic. I guess this all went to a real bad place."

Salvo folded his arms and tilted his head as he regarded the group in silence for a moment. "Well, I finally caught up with you brats," he mused. The mask was doing something to his voice. Devol had only heard the man talk briefly before and his voice had been arrogant and a little shrill. He could still hear that but it was like another voice overlapped with his, this one monotone and almost grave.

"I had hoped to find that mori here but guess he thought this wasn't worth his time, huh?" He pointed his wand at the pit. "But I guess he doesn't have to watch over you. You have that big fella with you—down there I'm guessing? It sure looks like he would be a fun match."

"If you couldn't take Vaust you can't take Wulfsun!" Devol cried heatedly. "They are equals in the order."

"Is that so?" Salvo chuckled and the unnerving voice echoed it. "Well, I look forward to seeing how long he can last against me. It'll give me some idea and a time to beat when I find the mori." He grinned, his wand still pointed at the pit. "But that's for later. Right now, I want to enjoy our reunion." A circle of fire erupted, covered the vast edge of the hole, and climbed a few feet.

Devol turned and tried to shout to Wulfsun but a blue light flashed behind him. He turned to see that Jazai had created a shield to block the attacks by the four ghouls that sprang into action as soon as he looked away.

"It won't hold!" the diviner shouted and Devol and Asla

prepared to fight as the shield fell and the beings pushed through.

Salvo watched this for a moment in genuine amusement. They had been able to hold Koli off so they should be able to last against a few ghouls for a couple of minutes, at least. He pointed Kapre above the pit and rolled the wand in his hands. He would need a little time to set this up, but it would be worth the effort. It was dark in this hole, after all.

CHAPTER TWENTY-EIGHT

Two ghouls, one with a pair of daggers and the other with wretched claws, clashed against Devol's sword. Asla battered one away and Jazai swept in quickly to grab the ghoul with the knives and ported them away.

Devol forced the remaining two back, slid away, and held his sword up. These beings were fast and much stronger than he had imagined. Wulfsun had said they were reanimated corpses, right? He would have thought their muscles would have decayed if that were the case. He studied them as they began to circle him and noticed that they pulsed with mana, but it didn't appear to be Salvo's. It couldn't be theirs as the dead could not form mana, and whoever gave it to them had enough to spare as these entities could use vis with ease.

He held his blade to one side and his gaze darted from one to the other. He glanced at Salvo, who waved his wand casually toward the pit, and he frowned. What was he doing? One of the ghouls moved toward him and he snapped to face it. He could fight multiple opponents at once usually, but given how fast these could move, if he messed up only once, that might give them enough of an opening to disembowel him. Instinctively, he began to back away, only to realize that would either take him closer to the crop fields and whatever might be lurking in there or closer to the fires Salvo had already created.

He looked at his teammates. Jazai managed to fend his opponent off but couldn't land a clean strike and Asla and her ghoul traded blows. It was fast enough to keep up with her, but she had been worn down by their time in the abyss. While he was certain she could outlast it, he wasn't sure how long it would take before she could eliminate it. Either way, neither of his friends could take one of his two adversaries. He needed to take care of these grunts and get to Salvo. His instincts didn't like that he merely stood there and made no effort to attack them as well given how much he seemed to want to hurt them.

The young swordsman looked at Achroma. It was a fine long blade but he would probably be better off at the moment with two shorter ones. The ghouls lunged at him, one on either side. He moved to defend against the one with daggers and would try to dodge the other, but he might have to take the blow. Seconds before they stuck, Achroma's light flashed. He held firm against the attacker's blades and anticipated the blow from the other one, but it never came. When he glanced back, he gaped in astonishment. The second being was held back by another sword shaped exactly like Achroma but made purely of the white light that ran through his blade.

Devol kicked the ghoul off him and the floating sword swiped at the other to force it back. He spun his sword and the duplicate copied his movement before it turned to face the other assassin. This was something new and very welcome at the moment. With more assuredness granted to him thanks to the magically appearing weapon, he lunged at the creature in front of him and the light sword attacked the other.

His adversary held its daggers up to block him but was no match against the heft and strength of his sword. He almost shattered the daggers with a strike and knocked the ghoul's hands away before he spun and used the momentum to carve through the creature's waist and slice it in two.

He turned to see the other trying to reach him, but the light sword no longer mirrored his actions and instead, tried to either attack it or simply held it at bay by deflecting it. Devol leapt forward and tried to run his blade through the creature's head but it caught his blade as he landed. He struggled against it for a moment, looked at the light blade, and smiled as he snatched it by the hilt and drove it into his adversary's stomach.

The ghoul's grasp weakened and he yanked his majestic out of its hands before he raised it high and arced it down through the creature's skull. As its body collapsed, black liquid seeped from its skin. The light sword vanished from his hands and he was baffled for a moment. He didn't want that to happen, he thought wildly. Then again, he did not know how it had appeared in the first place.

Devol looked at Jazai, who had finally trapped his opponent and weakened it with a shock cantrip before he used a mana blade to behead it. Asla was already finished. She tossed the head of her opponent to the side and he grinned. It appeared he was the only one to show any ingenuity in his finishing blows. He and the wildkin moved forward to confront Salvo, who had turned to look at them. The young swordsman felt a nervous chill despite the heat when he realized that the mask seemed to smile at him.

"Oh, no!" Jazai shouted and pointed frantically into the sky above the pit. "He's going to roast them!"

Asla and Devol whirled and both scowled at a large orb of flame far above, close to the top of the dome. The boy lunged at the fire magi before he could register what he was doing. He swung his blade over his head in preparation to strike Salvo down. Before he could complete the motion, the fire magi whipped a hand out and struck him across the face to hurl him several yards and close to the fire-wall. Asla managed to bound closer and stopped him.

Devol stared at the large man while he tried to regain his footing from the impact. Had he been that strong before? He did not remember fighting him physically but someone who used fire magic like that usually preferred to fight from a distance. They didn't train that much in physical combat. He and Asla glanced at one another while Salvo stared at his hand with his head tilted to one side. It appeared even he was rather impressed by how much power he had unleashed in one blow.

"Incredible isn't it?" the fire mage asked and returned his focus to the group. "I had heard about the malefics, even when I was your age, but never paid them much attention. They were powerful, sure, but the tradeoffs... Well, I was fine with Kapre when I eventually got my hands on her." He pointed the wand at the large fire orb and lowered it. The three friends watched in horror as the orb plummeted past the fire-wall and into the pit, which erupted in a pillar of flame.

"No! Wulfsun, Farah!" Devol shouted before the explosion knocked both him and Asla back. He turned to the fire magi with fury in his eyes. "Salvo!"

"So you are finally showing a little spirit!" The man laughed, waved his wand in front of him, and sent a whip of fire at the swordsman.

Jazai moved quickly in front of him and held a hand out. "Frost!" A wall of frost formed in front of the group which Salvo's flames made impact with and caused steam. "It's burning too fast," the diviner warned and he grasped his two teammates and blinked out of the way before the fire bored a hole in the ice.

Salvo winced and balled his hand so tightly that he realized he could potentially snap Kapre. Under normal circumstances, that wasn't a concern but given his new accessory and the unnatural strength it gave him, it was a real and potentially fatal mistake. He ran a hand down the mask for a moment as the order from before grew steadily louder. *Kill them.* He would, of course. That was what he had come there to do, but he should take the time to enjoy it at least.

CHAPTER TWENTY-NINE

"By the Astrals, I hate doing that," Jazai said where he sprawled on the ground, coughed, and shook his head. "Teleporting oneself is enough of a pain but bringing others along for the ride makes things...whirly."

"Are you okay?" Asla asked and rubbed his back. "You did the same thing with the ghoul earlier."

"I had to get it out of the way," he muttered and rolled onto his knees. "I didn't want to have you dodging my attacks while dealing with the creep."

"Where did you take us?" Devol asked and looked around. "Are we in the crops?"

"I didn't have time to plan." He raised a hand but lowered it weakly. "I chose a direction and cast us through the...the...hold on." Jazai slumped and moaned and Asla rubbed his back.

"We need to get him out of here." The young swordsman patted his friend's pocket. "Where's his marble?"

"No!" the diviner protested and forced himself to stand.

"We need to keep Salvo busy while Wulfsun and Farah finish with the rift."

"Wulfsun?" Devol asked incredulously. "Do you think he's all right?"

Both his friends shook their heads. "What? Of course! You haven't learned yet that surviving perilous situations is simply what he does?"

***

"What in the hells was that?" the Templar roared, pushed himself to his feet, and helped Farah to stand. Above them, a massive dome created using his majestic had defended them from the large fireball that threatened to incinerate them. All around the barrier, the pit was aflame but inside their smaller space, they were safe. "Damn. I had to let go of the rift to make that barrier."

"Is it opening again?" Farah asked and glanced at the portal "Can you still close it?"

"Aye, but I need to keep this barrier going as well," he stated and studied the inferno outside their haven. "Those aren't normal, even for magic fire. I don't want to risk being caught in that."

"Wulfsun!" Farah held her blade up and nodded toward the portal. Several more fiends came through, these a little more solidly built than the gaunt horde they had recently fought. "Focus on the rift. I'll take care of these."

"Thanks." Wulfsun nodded. "I'll work as fast as I can. The barrier will probably get smaller if I have to keep it up for too long. And when we're done..." He looked into the sky. "We need to find out whatever the hell made that fire. Hopefully, the young ones don't do anything rash."

Salvo strolled around the fire-wall and threw out small blasts of flame in an attempt to smoke the three friends out. "Have you left already?" he shouted and set fire to a row of crops. "Is this getting too hot for you?" He sighed at that. It was pathetic. He could usually come up with better taunts but he was too hot and bothered. What the hells was wrong with him?

He looked at the fire-wall around the pit, parted a section slightly, and peered in. At the very bottom, a dome of bright yellow light was visible amongst the fire. A magical shield? It must have been damn sturdy to survive his attack and still be standing. He squinted at the numerous figures inside. One wielded a sword and fought several darker humanoid beings. A larger one occasionally confronted a few of the creatures but seemed to be focused on something to do with the rift.

It didn't matter to him exactly what they were doing. He had tried to kill them earlier and it would be bad form to let them continue living. It was a point of pride with him to finish what he started if possible. He pointed his wand at the shield and considered the best way to destroy it when he sensed a powerful surge of mana directed toward him.

"Salvo!" Devol roared and raced toward the fire magi with renewed vigor.

"There you are," he responded cheerfully, turned

toward him, and fired a stream of flames. The boy swung his blade to cut them cleanly and disperse them. The fire magi leapt aside and the blade narrowly missed his jacket. "You can cut through fire?" he asked. "Is that normal for a sword?"

"Frost!" Jazai shouted and a pillar of ice suddenly encased all but the bottom of his left leg, right arm, and neck.

"Do you think this can hold me, you novice?" he demanded as he began to force out of the ice using his strength alone.

"Fortify!" the diviner stated calmly. The ice began to harden and compress the villainous magi.

"Clever little bastard." Salvo scowled and tried to spin his wand in his hand. As he began to form a fireball to blast himself out, Asla pounced at him, her claws extended and aimed at his mask. "Don't you dare, mongrel!" He hissed his outrage and the fire orb turned into several smaller ones that he cast at her. She was able to twist around them and stretch a claw forward to swipe as he managed to burst through the ice in a fit of rage. The wildkin rebounded off the pillar, which began to melt from the heat, and landed near Devol as the fire magi landed and ran a hand over his mask. He suddenly became very still.

The young swordsman noted marks on the mask. Asla had been able to damage it, although the plan was for her to try to steal it. He would finish it, he decided. That had to at least cause some damage to Salvo, shouldn't it? They were connected as long as he wore it. He took Achroma in both hands and the light within swirled into a fire not unlike his adversary's. As the man turned toward him, he surged into an attack. Thick, deep-red blood poured from the marks on the mask and it now pulsated.

"You dare too?" Salvo growled his outrage and raised his wand as Devol arced his blade. "I am done playing." He cast out a large torrent of fire as the boy unleashed the same from his blade, similar to the attack he had used against Koli months before. These flames, however, did not tear through the land like those had. Instead, they were halted and clashed against his adversary's inferno, one that slowly changed color to an unnatural crimson hue.

"Devol!" Asla cried and prepared to run toward him, only for the flames around the pit to flare out in front of her and block her path. Jazai used his frost cantrip to create paths between the flames but they melted faster than he could make them.

The young swordsman's hands shook and the flames from his blade were forced back and he along with them. The fire magi's continued to grow as he stalked forward. "This is what forced Koli to run?" he shouted over the roar of the flames. "Pathetic!"

Jazai eased behind Devol and threw up a large wall of ice before he stretched forward and yanked the swordsman back. Salvo screamed at them and his fire blazed through the frigid wall in one swipe. The diviner jumped and moved both of them out of the way as the crimson flames seared the ground along its path.

With a yell, he threw his robes off and Devol realized they were alight. His friend fumbled on his belt, retrieved a vial of clear liquid, and poured it along his arm where burn marks were visible from his knuckles to his shoulder. "Jazai!"

"I'll be fine!" The boy grunted and flexed his hand. "The fire burns like the hells, though. What was with that color?"

"It has to be something to do with the mask," Devol reasoned. "Check your tome."

Jazai opened the book as the two boys wandered around the labyrinth of flames in search of an escape "It won't tell us anything," the diviner stated and his lips pressed together in frustration.

"Is he blocking you somehow?" he asked.

"No, it's not that." His friend flipped the book and showed it to him. "I don't think he's capable of anything like that now."

Devol looked at the page which contained no paragraphs and no general information, only two pages filled with the same words constantly repeated. *Burn them, kill them, consume them.*

CHAPTER THIRTY

"That mask is taking its toll," Jazai stated and shut his tome. "It grants power in many ways and forms, but each time you use it, the cost is a little more of your sanity. It doesn't take long to collect, especially if you weren't all there to begin with."

"Consume?" Devol sliced through the lines of fire with his blade. "Does he want to eat us?"

"I wouldn't put it past him at this point." The diviner placed his hand against his burn and used frost to wrap it in ice. "I'm not sure if that is his desire or some kind of condition of using the mask. Or maybe he's simply losing it, but I'm not interested enough to find out."

"Asla!" Devol shouted and swept his blade through more flame. "Asla, where are—" His words died as the fire began to die down before it pulled away from the ground entirely and floated above them, where it contorted and formed into separate strands.

The wildkin stared at the flames much like they did before they all looked at Salvo, who held his wand straight up to the sky. Devol's gaze shifted to the mask. It was still bleeding and its form had shifted again so it lived up to its name. The man looked like a demon—or, rather, like he was possessed by one. He no longer bellowed or screamed but wordlessly pointed his wand at them as the flames coiled around one another to form a serpentine figure.

The fire magi whipped the wand toward them and the fiery snake struck out at them. The swordsman ran forward and attempted to block the attack with Achroma. He succeeded once and knocked the snake to the side, but the man simply flicked the wand in the other direction and the serpent attacked, surged into his sword, and dislodged it from his hand.

Asla's anima flared and she prepared to strike while Jazai tended to Devol, but the fire creature encircled all three of them and constricted quickly around them. "Keep your animas up!" Jazai shouted and uttered a hiss of pain as the snake inched closer to his burned arm. Devol reached for his majestic but the snake was too quick, ensnared the trio, and hoisted them into the air.

The fire's form was almost crystalline and bound them together to take this shape and hold them. Devol could feel the heat burning him even with his anima holding it at bay. He tried to reach into his pocket but he couldn't. From this position, he couldn't even reach his marble. In his panic, he didn't think to call his majestic to him.

Salvo wanted to taunt them and ask if they regretted their choice to try to be Templars and if they wondered if they had made any progress at all if they died so young because of foolish choices. But instead, he heard the incessant demand in his head—*burn them, kill them, consume them*. He wanted to and could sense that the desire was his own, but it also felt wrong—like he was rushing this. After all his efforts, he wanted to enjoy it more but the voice constantly demanded and ordered and he could not hold against it.

"I can't...get my majestic!" Devol cried and as common sense kicked in, he stretched his hand out and attempted to summon it to him. It was one of the tricks he had mastered, he believed, but with the heat and pain, he could not focus.

"I can't blink us out of here!" Jazai warned and squirmed in the fiery serpent's grasp. "It's taking all my mana simply to fight against it."

"I have...I have a way out," Asla shouted and the boys immediately looked at her. "I cannot promise I will be able to help after but I can do this much."

"Asla, what are you talking about?" Devol's question got a response from her in the form of action. Her anima flared again and the cat silhouette that would appear around her body during intense fights began to solidify and become more than a mere shadow. The snake seemed to weaken as she began to push it apart. The form of a tiger or panther surrounded her now and it dug its claws into the snake and ripped it apart. Asla snapped her head toward the serpent's, her fangs protruding, and bit the creature's head, yanked it back, and ripped it off. The rest of it disintegrated and released them to fall heavily.

"Asla!" Devol yelled and stared at where she lay unmoving on the ground. Jazai went to examine her quickly and nodded to him that she was breathing at least.

"No!" The two turned to Salvo, who had begun to

create a fireball. "No, no, no!" The swordsman snatched Achroma up as the man fired volley after volley at them. He knocked each fiery missile to the side or into the air. As the fire magi prepared to launch a much larger fireball, he reared and held the blade up, then swung it forward. It immediately brightened and created an extended blade of light that cleaved through the infernal orb and struck Salvo's wand.

A loud crack heralded the shattered pieces of the red crystal that fell around the man, and a furious, pained scream followed. As the fireball erupted to scatter fire around the area, blood spilled from under Salvo's mask and a large wound stained his shirt. Majestics were connected to their users and their destruction was the owner's pain. The man fell to one knee, his breathing ragged, and for the first time in their fight, he truly looked vulnerable. He turned to Devol and the mask began to pulsate again as the features shifted into an expression of wrath.

"Jazai, you and Asla get out of here," he said quietly and spun his sword.

"No way. I'm not leaving until I see this bastard fall." Jazai replied although he took a moment to look at the unconscious wildkin. Devol realized that staying might be for the best at that moment.

"Then watch over her," he requested, drew a deep breath, and readied his sword. "I will end this."

Salvo uttered another angry yell and smacked his wand into the ground. Even without the crystal, a column of flame erupted around him. Jazai summoned a shield as the swordsman held his blade up and occasionally deflected errant blasts of fire.

"He's losing it!" the diviner shouted and strengthened his shield. "Way more than he has already."

"I can't fight him at this range." Devol began to move forward. "I need to get in close!"

"Then take this!" Jazai tossed him a vial of the blue liquid he had poured on himself. "It's for magical burns. Pour some on your hands and lower arms and you may be able to buy more time to get a good strike."

Devol nodded, popped the top of the vial, and applied the liquid as suggested. He tossed the vial aside and lunged toward Salvo, who now turned to face him. The fire magi swung his wand and the column around him spread wider. The boy planted his blade into the ground as he had seen Farah do. He created a barrier in front of him that took the hit but the force was still enough to almost knock him back if he hadn't had such a tight hold on his majestic.

Quickly, he yanked it out of the ground and continued his onslaught. Salvo, at this point, merely slung his wand around almost as if it were a blade to cast random fireballs and blasts of flame in his direction. The young swordsman dodged easily or parried most of these until he finally moved close enough for him to charge his blade and make a desperate move to end this by driving it into his adversary. But before it could connect, a massive wall of fire formed in front of the psychotic magi and held his blade in place as it formed into the same crystal-like form as the snake earlier.

The boy was able to pry his sword out of the fire and he jumped back. The serpentine shape wavered and shifted into what he had stared at during this entire fight. He grimaced as it took on the form of the demon mask, although this one had an open maw where orbs of fire danced within.

A voice spoke but it did not sound like Salvo's. Instead, the dark, grave voice that had seemed to underpin the fire magi's speech took control, although it was now loud and cavernous. It echoed the words from the pages of Jazai's tome...*consume, consume, consume.* As Devol stared at the fiery recreation of the malefic, he felt for a brief moment that the dark desire might come to pass.

CHAPTER THIRTY-ONE

Farah smashed the pommel of her blade into the face of one of the fiends and raised a shield hastily as two others attempted to strike her from behind. She turned and cut through them before she flipped her blade and drove it through the attacker behind her. "How much longer, Wulfsun?"

"I almost have it!" the Templar shouted. The rift had narrowed to such an extent that he could grasp it with his actual gauntlets. He looked at a fiend that tried to force itself through the shrinking portal and with a grimace, he lifted his leg and stamped his boot on it to knock it back. "Get out of here, you annoyin' inkblot!"

"The barrier is shrinking again," Farah announced when she noticed the edges continue to close in around her. She kicked another of the beings into it before she thrust her enchanted sword through it. The blow eliminated the fiend but also cracked the barrier. "Hells! It's weakening too."

"I only need a few more minutes," Wulfsun promised.

"Once I collapse it enough, I can make the ward It won't take but a jif."

"Will that also take care of the dome?" she asked as she looked around her. The fiends had finally been worn down enough that they no longer regenerated.

"The ward will reverse the magic and keep the rift closed, and abyssal magic will either disperse or be reabsorbed into its realm," the Templar explained and pulled the edges of the rift closer with the gauntlets of his majestic. "We need to destroy those obelisks as well and keep fragments to see if we can determine where they came from."

"Is there anything I can do to help? The fiends seem to be gone for now," she told him, although she refused to put her sword away for the moment.

"Aye, you can start making the ward." Wulfsun grunted and strained to seal the last sections of the rift. "Take the powder out of my satchel and make a ring around the rift."

Farah ran up behind him and paused when she saw three satchels. "Which one?"

"In a flask...the satchel above the left cheek," the man snapped and his gauntlets grew brighter as he clenched his teeth. "Hurry! I want to get back to the kids."

She found the flask, opened it, and ran quickly around the rift, leaving a trail of the powder behind her. "When yer done, I need you to create a shield to protect us from the fire. I need to drop my barrier to focus on containing the rift while I finish the ward. Do you have enough mana left for that?"

"I do," she assured him, reached the end of the circle,

and hurried to his side with the flask ready. "Tell me when."

Wulfsun nodded and opened his palms as the rift condensed even further. He maneuvered around it and shaped it into an orb the size of a grapefruit. "All right, I'm preparing to drop my barrier. You're up!"

Farah held her sword aloft and a stream of light magic poured out and formed around them as his barrier fell. He created a small barrier around the rift itself and took the flask out again as he backed away slowly. The magics of the rift thrust against his shielding. Quickly, he set to work finishing the ward and hurried as much as he could without making a mistake. Wards weren't his specialty, which made it a little more challenging. He took a moment to look at the fiery wall around the edges of the pit. It had been a while since he had spoken to any Astral, but he took a moment to threaten Finis and demanded that he not take the young ones. Otherwise, he would have to talk to him personally.

Devol showed no fear to his enemy, but it did no good. Salvo probably couldn't even see him through the inferno he had created. A torrent of flame streamed out of the mask and the boy turned his blade so the flat side faced forward and created a shield. The fire was relentless and pushed him back with its onslaught. The shield began to evaporate and he prepared to leap out of the way before it gave out completely. He jumped and expected to be scalded before a blue shield appeared as his gave way.

"Jazai!" he shouted, landed on his feet, and turned as the diviner's shield was smothered. His friend was on his knees with an arm extended. "Thank you, but you and Asla need to get out of here."

"I know...dammit!" Jazai muttered and fumbled in Asla's pocket to take her marble out. "That was the last of my mana. I barely have enough to be useful but you need to go too."

"I can't, not as long as—"

"Devol, look out!" The swordsman spun as several fire-balls streaked toward him. He blocked a couple of them but one caught him in the chest and set his jacket and shirt on fire. Hastily, he stripped them off and checked himself for wounds. Slight burns were visible on his chest and stomach but could have been much worse without his anima.

As he checked his waist, his hand touched an item he had forgotten about—one that gave him pause. He looked at the demonic visage in the fire-wall. "Jazai, I need to end this."

"Wulfsun will take care of him," the diviner protested. "Can you even get around him to—" Devol drew the item from his waist and held it behind his back for his friend to see. The boy understood almost immediately. "If you're gonna try that, you'd better make it count," he muttered as he retrieved his marble and held it in his hand. "We'll be waiting." Jazai poured mana into both marbles and his and Asla's forms vanished into a stream of mana that quickly moved through the dome.

"They can't run away!" Salvo shouted. The fire-wall parted and the man walked through. "I'll find them again after I deal with you. I will kill you all." At least he was now speaking in complete sentences again.

The boy stood and pointed his majestic at the fire magi. "You aren't leaving here, Salvo."

"Make your boasts," the man all but growled and whipped the fires around him into a frenzy. "Have you even killed a man before, brat? I've killed hundreds. Do you think I'll simply let you cut your teeth on me? I have a new world to see."

Devol made no answer as he slid his hand behind him. The fire magi prepared to send all the flames forward but the boy flung a dagger before he could do so. Salvo didn't need the enhancements from the mask to dodge it. He simply tilted his head to the right and let it sail past. He chuckled at what he considered a foolish final attempt to wound him.

But as he launched the massive waves of flames at the young Templar trainee, the boy disappeared. Salvo shuddered and turned when he felt a presence behind him. His adversary reappeared and before his feet even touched the ground, he struck out with his blade. Salvo snarled defiance and gathered the fire for another attack, but Achroma sank deep into his chest.

"Only a little longer!" Wulfsun shouted and placed his hands on the edge of the ward. "I'm activating it now." It glowed and turned the yellow of his mana. He dropped the protective shield around the rift and it began to stagnate and no longer pulsed with magic, although something dark flowed into it from above. He looked at a thin line of abyssal magic that came from the very top of the dome. It was able to funnel into the rift even through Farah's shield, and the strand continued to grow as the flow moved faster. "It's done!" he shouted and turned to the guard captain. "The abyssal magic is returning to its realm. We need to go."

"What about the rift?" she asked and pointed in alarm. "It's opening again."

The Templar turned and realized that it had indeed begun to open, but it was not growing. "The ward will keep it contained. We need to destroy the obelisks but it opened to absorb the magic coming in." He gestured around them. "Drop the shield and let's go."

Farah released her barrier and pointed to the top of the pit. "Those fires above are getting weaker." Wulfsun noticed that the once-raging flames had begun to shrink and flickered weakly. Something had happened above.

Devol moved to pull his blade out of Salvo but the man stumbled back and removed the blade himself. He looked at the wound and shook visibly, either in shock or rage. The boy held Achroma in one hand, breathing heavily, and he grimaced at the blade coated by his adversary's blood.

The fire magi began to chuckle and looked slowly at him. "A nice...hit," he muttered and coughed. Fresh drops of blood came from beneath the mask, "How does it feel? To kill a man?" The boy did not answer and simply gazed at him with contempt, although there was a brief flicker of concern that set the maniac off. "Relish it! Don't you balk now, coward!" he screamed and the voice of the mask fell away. "Do you think I'm the worst this realm has to offer? You had best get used to this if you dare to stand up to him."

"To who?" Devol demanded. "Who are you working for?"

Salvo lurched forward but stopped himself and began to laugh again. "It doesn't matter. I won't see the new world but neither will you." With a shaking hand, he began to point his wand at the boy, who did not respond by lifting his blade. Instead, he dropped it, rushed forward, and focused the rest of his mana on vis as he balled his fist. He drove it into the mask and the blow catapulted the man back. Fragments of the mask shattered and splintered off.

The fire magi fell through the fires around the pit as Wulfsun and Farah leapt up. They spun as he passed them and Devol ran to the edge and watched as he fell into the bottom of the pit and directly into the portal. The man reached a hand up as the rift seemed to yawn hungrily and the bottom half of his body sank immediately into the rift. A chunk of the mask was destroyed and revealed one eye that showed, anger, confusion, and fear.

As Salvo slid into the abyss and it shrank behind him, the Templar pointed to the obelisks, whose runes were now blank. "Farah!"

"I'm on it." She picked her sword up, enchanted it with light, and swiped at the air to create a magical projectile that cut one of the obelisks in half. She swung her arm and destroyed the other, which shattered and spat pieces in every direction. "Devol, you have your marble, right?"

He checked his pants pocket and took it out. "I do," he said as Wulfsun retrieved his as he stooped to take something off the ground.

"We need to leave. Use it," she ordered and immediately disappeared in a flash of mana.

Devol looked at his mentor, who nodded to him with a solemn expression. "Come on, lad. We should talk." With that, they activated their marbles as the dome continued to shrink and the magics returned to their rightful dimension.

CHAPTER THIRTY-TWO

When Wulfsun and Devol escaped the dome, they were greeted by corpses and fire. "Aw, hells." The Templar grunted and scowled regretfully at some of the fallen. "I should have realized."

"Wulfsun!" Farah shouted and gestured for him to join a small group. "There are survivors."

"I'll be right there." He placed a large hand on the boy's shoulder. "You did good, lad. I'll talk to you in a moment but you should check in with your friends, yeah?"

"Yeah." He nodded and looked for Jazai and Asla. They were farther down the field near the hills and he rushed to them. The diviner was tending Asla's wounds. "Hey, are you guys all right?"

The other boy nodded silently at first before he looked briefly away from his work. "Did you get him?"

Devol drew a deep breath and nodded. "I did."

"What happened?" Asla asked when she saw the burns on his body. "Are you all right?"

"I'll be fine after I see a healer," he assured them and

traced a hand over his wounds. "As for what happened, I was able to get around him." He took the dagger out. "Using Rogo's gift, I was able to get a hit." He placed a hand carefully on his chest. "Right through his chest."

"Did you get the heart?" Jazai inquired as he stared at his friend's blade and noted the drying blood.

Devol fell back a little in surprise. "As in...ripped it out?"

"What? No! I mean, did you—" He stopped and sighed as he shook his head. "Never mind. I'm only making sure he's dead."

"Well, he was bleeding badly." The swordsman sat next to his friends, took his sheathed sword off his back, and placed it beside him. "And the sword ran him through. After that, I knocked him into the rift."

"You knocked him into it?" Asla asked, her voice still a little faint as she attempted to sit.

Devol looked at his hand. "It wasn't my plan but he attempted to attack me and... Well, I hit him with enough power to push him into the pit and he fell into the rift as Wulfsun and Farah finished shutting it."

"Trapped in the Abyss?" Jazai looked at the dome, which was now not even a fourth of the size it had been when they first arrived. "I would prefer a body, but there ain't a chance he can make it out of that. Even if he had a marble or something to teleport to our realm, they don't work in the Abyss. At least, that's what Zier told me."

"So, it's over then?" Asla asked and her gaze settled on the dome. "We won?"

The swordsman gave her a wide and very tired grin as he stood. "Yeah, we did. We helped close the rift and we were able to…to…" He wavered and his sight grew blurry for a moment. He stumbled and Jazai began to stand to steady him. Devol held a hand out to stop him, then placed it on his face and wiped the sweat off. He felt dampness around his eyes and realized they stung. For some unaccountable reason, he was tearing up.

These were tears of happiness, right? They had accomplished their mission, everyone was all right—injured but alive—and yet… He looked at the bodies of the scholars, guards, and soldiers burned by Salvo on his way inside. The fire magi had said that he had killed hundreds during his life. He was not a good person and was as much a monster as any Devol had fought or slain up to this point, But as his tears began to flow more freely and created tracks down his face, he looked at his blood-soaked majestic.

Asla waved someone over as Jazai stood and walked closer to him. "Devol, what's wrong?"

"I…I don't…" he stammered and rubbed the tears from his face. "I don't know. G-give me a minute."

"Asla, Jazai, how are ye?" Wulfsun asked as he strode up to the group. "Good job holding off that bastard and making it out. Do you need—" Asla stopped him with a shake of her head and pointed at Devol.

The Templar needed no explanation. He merely nodded and moved to the boy, who tried to dry his tears. "Hey, lad, come with me for a moment," he said and placed a hand gently on his back. The young swordsman nodded and slid Achroma into its scabbard as they wandered to the other side of the hill.

The silence hung between them as they walked. Devol

looked over his shoulders at the small group of survivors. "Are they okay?"

Wulfsun noted the direction of his gaze and nodded. "Some have injuries and a couple of the scholars are still in shock. None of them were prepared for something that brutal." He sighed and ran a hand through his wild mane of hair. "Unfortunately, that's the world we live in, though. There are many bastards like fire magi out there."

"Salvo," he replied and focused on the dome, which was now about the size of a house. The area it had possessed remained withered. "He was one of the magi who attacked us during our mission in Rouxwoods."

"I remember Vaust talking about him," the Templar said quietly. "That mask of his…was that a malefic?"

"Yes." Devol stopped beside a group of bushes. "It was… alive, I think. There was another presence in Salvo and he became more and more erratic as we fought."

"I've not seen it before but I've heard about it—the demon mask." Wulfsun folded his arms as he looked into the sky where dawn had begun to break. "You know, the first time I ever heard about it was when it was used in battle. A soldier and his squad were pinned down by a cult of some kind causing trouble in Britana. During a raid, the soldiers were able to snatch the mask, although they had no idea what it was.

"While they were under siege, a soldier put it on and he was able to wipe out the cultists in a matter of a couple of minutes and saved his team." He sighed, closed his eye, and shook his head. "In the end, though, the mask continued to call to him even after he took it off. He stole it from the same military stronghold he had turned it in to only a week before. His body was found a few months later in a cave, scrawny and pale. Locals from the village near the cave said they heard odd screams at night, most likely from him. They never recovered the mask after that."

"Do you think Salvo killed him for it?" Devol asked as images of the mask appeared in his mind.

"That is doubtful. Vaust said Salvo told him about how he got his wand by stealing it from his master. The last time anyone had seen the mask was more than a decade ago and he would have probably still been an apprentice at the time. My guess is whoever he worked for had it done or did it themselves." He eyed the young magi with concern. "Did he say anything about that, boyo?"

"Working with someone?" the boy asked and tried to recall. "Besides Koli—the other thief from before— I can't remember anyone else. But he kept saying he would see a 'new world' or something like that."

"A new world eh?" Wulfsun stroked his beard, his expression thoughtful. "I've heard proclamations like that all too often in my time, and it is always some nutter yelling it." He looked at the young man whose face was still forlorn and he sighed as he lowered his hand and knelt so that they were similar in height. Gently, he turned to young magi toward him. "Tell me...what are you feeling, lad?"

Devol looked at the abyss again. It was all but gone and the small gathering on the hill paused to watch as the last of the anomaly was absorbed into the portal before the rift disappeared.

"He's gone for good now." He drew his majestic and looked at the blood on the blade. Absently, he fumbled in one of his pouches to find a cloth to wipe it with but it must have fallen out during the fighting.

His companion deduced this, removed a soft gray cloth from his pouch, and handed it to the boy, who took it and attempted to clean the blade. "I shouldn't be so bothered," Devol muttered, his voice low and quiet. "He was a killer and proud of it. His boast was that he came here to kill me, my friends, you, Vaust...anyone—" He stopped wiping his weapon almost as soon as he had begun and lowered his head. "And yet I can't...I can't stop shaking now."

Wulfsun studied the boy. Indeed, his hands shook although it was subtle. Years of swordplay had driven the need for self-control into him, but he could not stop this. The man placed a massive paw on top of his hands to steady them and Devol realized that for all the fire he had recently dealt with, he was cold.

"It is all right," the Templar said and gave him a moment to breathe. "Those of us who have been in battle for so long take the innocence we once had for granted. I had hoped to prepare you myself for the actions you would have to take in this profession."

"I should have been ready," the swordsman interrupted and his voice cracked. "I was! I ran him through—he left me no choice!" He turned his blade and drove it into the earth. "I had planned to be a guard and read stories of knights and heroes who vanquished evil-doers with their might. I knew I would have to do so myself, no matter what path I chose." He tightened his grasp on the hilt of his sword. "Why does this bother me? He was nothing more than evil. He was—"

"Human," Wulfsun said quietly to end his tirade. "That's

the thing, Devol. Even with everything he was at the core, it can be easier to accept the death of a monster that has scales and claws than one with flesh and a visage like yours." He stood and drew a deep breath. "I killed my first man—well, first three—when I was about a year or so older than you. It was during a scouting mission on some bandits that went tits-up. We weren't even supposed to confront them and had been ordered to report them to local guards. But I guess I wasn't built for stealth, even as a boy. In a way, I was lucky. Not only was I trained all my life to fight like my life depended on it, but I was so busy trying to fight within the chaos that it didn't hit me until it was all over."

Devol nodded and rubbed his eyes. "I feel the same way. It wasn't until I saw him sink into that portal that I truly understood what I had done."

The Templar folded his arms, his expression one of understanding. "In the end, I threw myself into my training and snuck some alcohol in from time to time, but I didn't let it linger. I don't recommend that, however. It led me to be...not myself for a while." He straightened, took a few steps in front of the boy, and turned to him. "Devol, you must understand that neither I nor anyone in the order wants to force this life upon you. You have been a great help and will do incredible things no matter where you go. If you need to find another—"

"I will not." As he looked at his mentor with determination in his eyes, Devol said, "I am—will be—a Templar. I know this will not be the last time I will have to strike down other magi like myself, but I will not let that stop me.

I know I can do…I can help more here than anywhere else. I believe that."

Wulfsun considered this a for a moment before he placed a large hand on his shoulder. "I'm glad you feel that way, lad, but I know it hurts. Your first kill will always be something that shakes your foundation. But understand the fact that you can care about someone like him—an evil magi who wished to do you and your friends harm—and still choose to confront him and do what needed to be done. That is a strength that it takes most people years to come to terms with, if they ever do. I'm proud of you, boyo. You did well."

Devol nodded and a few tears spilled as he smiled a little less shakily. "Thank you, sir."

"Is everything all right?" Asla asked as she and Jazai joined them. "Farah is asking for you, Wulfsun."

The Templar nodded. "She probably needs me for her report. I'm praying to the Astrals that she won't make me talk to her boss again." He sighed and scratched his chin. "I'll go and deal with that and hopefully, we can find an inn and get some rest before we return to the order hall." He took a few steps away but paused for a moment to turn to them and smile. "You all did well. Thanks for watching my back."

"Of course," Jazai responded with a weary but earnest grin. "I wouldn't want to be the one to have to explain to Zier why you didn't make it back. He'd find a way to blame me for it."

Wulfsun laughed and continued his walk to Farah. "I wouldn't worry about that," he quipped over his shoulder.

"He'll be too busy coming up with chores for you to pay it much mind."

The diviner shrugged as watched the giant man. "He's not wrong." He shook his head and turned his attention to Devol. "All right, tell the truth this time. Are you all right?"

The swordsman shook his head, pulled Achroma out of the ground, and rested it over his shoulder. "Yes…yes, I am." He looked at both of his friends gratefully. "Thank you for your help. I couldn't have handled him on my own."

"No kidding." Jazai looked at his burn marks and sighed. "I gotta be all nice about this. I honestly intended to give you an earful about making me leave you behind."

"You did?" Devol asked. "Jazai, that wasn't because I thought you couldn't handle it. Besides, you said yourself you were low on mana."

"I know, that's why I'm not all that pissed about it." He sighed and placed a hand on Asla's shoulder. "Honestly, we would have been done for if it wasn't for Asla's little trick back there."

"Right," he agreed when he recalled the form she had taken. "What was that, Asla? Some part of your majestic?"

The wildkin nodded. "It allows me to tap into my more animalistic side if I concentrate and increase the ability by overcharging my anima, and it almost allows me to shapeshift in a way." She frowned slightly. "Although it has its drawbacks, as you saw. I wasn't much good in the fight afterward."

"Trust me. You did your part," Jazai assured her.

Devol thought about that moment in the fight. "I couldn't reach my majestic and I couldn't call it to me.

There was nothing I could do." He smiled at her. "You saved us there, Asla."

She turned away, a little bashful. "I'm glad I could—" Her eyes widened. "Look!"

The boys turned their gaze to the bushes, where dozens of small, six-petaled red flowers with crimson veins had begun to bloom. Jazai walked closer and touched one. "Are these…"

"Bloodflowers." Asla nodded. "They are in bloom."

Devol looked down and realized that more flowers blossomed around them, even through the scorched earth. "They bloom when one person has killed another," he stated and turned to look at her "That was the story, right?"

She looked at the flowers, then slowly at him with concern in her eyes. "Yes, but that's only folklore, Devol."

The wind picked up and petals began to scatter. Jazai stepped away from the bushes. "Some of these are breaking apart."

They all stood in silence as the petals filled the air. The sun was rising in the east and the dawn light glimmered on some of the ascending petals. "I hope it is more than folklore," Devol replied and turned to them. "After all, Asla, you said you liked the bloodflowers because they reminded you that beauty could come from even dark moments, right?"

She stared at him for a moment, surprised that he recalled that. Jazai folded his arms and smirked. She looked at the petals and smiled. "That's right. I do believe that."

"And I want to believe that too," Devol replied, shifted his sword, and replaced it in its scabbard. "From now on, it is something I will always remember so I can carry on."

The story continues with The Oblivion Trials, available at Amazon and through Kindle Unlimited

Grab your copy today!

Thank you for not only reading this story but these notes as well.

So, I just got off a story call with an author, and we were discussing the difference between accurate and enjoyable.

(This is for a story that has not come out yet.)

We are in the second book of the series, about twenty-two chapters out of twenty-eight developed. The main protagonist and his two friends are having trouble because the "big guy" is acting pompous and makes all the decisions.

I realized while reading the latest chapters that I'm getting to the point where I'm, like, "You know what? Go ahead and be a @%@!#% and just die already."

Not the right way to feel about the main character.

So, the author and I jumped on a call to hash it out. She made a good point. Her husband is ex-military, so she is very aware of how it might go with someone who mimics the main character in real life.

Unfortunately, actions that are plausible and highly likely to occur can be annoying to read about.

At least, if you don't provide enough realization to the main character (read "annoying jerk") to allow us to emphasize with their decisions. It took us about fifteen minutes to figure out how we could implement the reality of the main character's actions while not making him a total a##hole at the same time.

The learning moment for me was a realization that what I was feeling was a discussion point related to the story from enjoyment and the publishing side, which is: *If it isn't enjoyable, we are unlikely to sell the next story in the series.*

Many authors I've met over the years don't stop to consider the enjoyment aspects of their stories. If a character is a jerk, or is one-dimensional, or kicks dogs (I don't suggest this), most readers are going to close the book and grab the next one (not that author's).

As a reader, if I wanted more reality, I could get that without getting lost in a book.

There are whole tropes where the main characters are jerks and sell very well. In romance, there is a trope called "jerk with a heart of gold." The purpose of the story is the female lead will uncover and allow the heart of gold to shine forth. You can't very well accomplish a great change if they aren't a jerk to begin with.

The Empire of Man series by David Weber and John Ringo starts with a main character who is a spoiled prince. Mind you, there are reasons he's a jerk. It is justified.

But had I read book 01 first, I never would have gone far enough to enjoy his turnaround. It so happens I read book 02 in the series, where he was already a good guy. I went back to read book one, and it was a struggle to deal with his crass behavior even when I knew how it turned out.

I'm just one of those readers who can't enjoy that type of scene.

We did solve the challenge with the story by weaving in a few more aspects of why he was acting the way he was. It allowed us to show a bit more of his humanity during jerk moments, and I believe it will carry the reader along to the natural conclusion where the relationships are all worked out.

Which is good. I like the character and really didn't want to be good with him dying.

Just to be clear, this particular issue wasn't a challenge with the co-author on this book.

I hope you have a fantastic week, or weekend, or holiday...or night if it's time to sleep!

Ad Aeternitatem,

Michael Anderle

CONNECT WITH MICHAEL

Connect with Michael Anderle

Website: http://lmbpn.com

Email List: http://lmbpn.com/email/

Social Media:

https://www.facebook.com/LMBPNPublishing

https://twitter.com/MichaelAnderle

https://www.instagram.com/lmbpn_publishing/

https://www.bookbub.com/authors/michael-anderle